Timber Falls Courier

MORE MYSTERY SHROUDS TIMBER FALLS!

FAMOUS PHOTOGRAPHER GOES HEAD-TO-HEAD WITH HOAX BUSTER

by Charity Jenkins

Something is afoot in Timber Falls—and it isn't Bigfoot. The world thought her father was a crackpot, but famous outdoor photographer Rozalyn Sawyer has come back to town to prove them wrong.

Back for the first time since her mother's tragic death ten years ago, Rozalyn has no idea what she's up against.

This reporter has learned that Ford Lancaster, the infamous scientist and Bigfoot hoax buster, was seen at Betty's Café. What could have brought this tall, dark and intense hunk to town? Is it possible Ford Lancaster is on the trail of Bigfoot? Or is he on a collision course with Rozalyn Sawyer? Never fear, this reporter, Charity Jenkins, will get to the bottom of it.

Dear Harlequin Intrigue Reader,

We have a superb lineup of outstanding romantic suspense this month starting with another round of QUANTUM MEN from Amanda Stevens. A *Silent Storm* is brewing in Texas and it's about to break....

More great series continue with Harper Allen's MEN OF THE DOUBLE B RANCH trilogy. *A Desperado Lawman* has his hands full with a spitfire who is every bit his match. As well, B.J. Daniels adds the second installment to her CASCADES CONCEALED miniseries with *Day of Reckoning*.

In *Secret Witness* by Jessica Andersen, a woman finds herself caught between a rock—a killer threatening her child—and a hard place—the detective in charge of the case. What will happen when she has to make the most inconceivable choice any woman can make?

Launching this month is a new promotion we are calling COWBOY COPS. Need I say more? Look for *Behind the Shield* by veteran Harlequin Intrigue author Sheryl Lynn. And newcomer, Rosemary Heim, contributes to DEAD BOLT with *Memory Reload*.

Enjoy!

Sincerely,

Denise O'Sullivan
Senior Editor
Harlequin Intrigue

DAY OF RECKONING

B.J. DANIELS

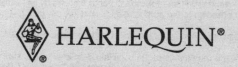

HARLEQUIN®

TORONTO • NEW YORK • LONDON
AMSTERDAM • PARIS • SYDNEY • HAMBURG
STOCKHOLM • ATHENS • TOKYO • MILAN • MADRID
PRAGUE • WARSAW • BUDAPEST • AUCKLAND

ISBN 0-373-22761-2

DAY OF RECKONING

Copyright © 2004 by Barbara Heinlein

This edition published by arrangement with Harlequin Books S.A.

Visit us at www.eHarlequin.com

Printed in U.S.A.

ABOUT THE AUTHOR

A former award-winning journalist, B.J. Daniels had thirty-six short stories published before her first romantic suspense, *Odd Man Out,* came out in 1995. In 2002 her books *Premeditated Marriage* and *Rodeo Daddy* were nominated for a Career Acheivement Award. B.J. lives in Montana with her husband, Parker, two springer spaniels, Zoey and Scout, and a temperamental tomcat named Jeff. She is a member of Kiss of Death, the Bozeman Writers Group and Romance Writers of America. When she isn't writing, she snowboards in the winters and camps and boats in the summers. All year she plays her favorite sport, tennis. To contact her, write P.O. Box 183, Bozeman, MT 59771 or visit her Web site at www.bjdaniels.com.

Books by B.J. Daniels

HARLEQUIN INTRIGUE
312—ODD MAN OUT
353—OUTLAWED!
417—HOTSHOT P.I.
446—UNDERCOVER CHRISTMAS
493—A FATHER FOR HER BABY
533—STOLEN MOMENTS
555—LOVE AT FIRST SIGHT
566—INTIMATE SECRETS
585—THE AGENT'S SECRET CHILD
604—MYSTERY BRIDE
617—SECRET BODYGUARD
643—A WOMAN WITH A MYSTERY
654—HOWLING IN THE DARKNESS
687—PREMEDITATED MARRIAGE
716—THE MASKED MAN
744—MOUNTAIN SHERIFF*
761—DAY OF RECKONING*

*Cascades Concealed

Portland •

Eugene •

PACIFIC OCEAN

Coos Bay •

Oakridge •

Timber Falls •

Cascade Mountain Range

OREGON

All underlined places are fictitious.

CAST OF CHARACTERS

Rozalyn Sawyer—She thinks all she has to fear in Timber Falls are the ghosts of her past. She can't be more wrong.

Ford Lancaster—All he cares about is money and fame—until he meets Rozalyn Sawyer.

Anna Sawyer—Her daughter Rozalyn is still haunted by her mother's suicide from the attic widow's walk ten years ago.

Liam Sawyer—Rozalyn's father is missing—and so soon after his quickie marriage to a younger woman. Is he really out hunting for Bigfoot? Or has he met with foul play?

Emily Lane Sawyer—She seems to be the perfect wife. Maybe too perfect?

Drew Lane—He's the only one of Rozalyn's new stepsiblings who seems to like her. But is it only to irritate his mother?

Suzanne Lane—Why does she feel the need to numb her senses with alcohol?

Dr. James Morrow—He was the last person to see Rozalyn's mother alive. And now no one has seen him for the past ten years.

Lynette Hargrove—The nurse bears a remarkable resemblance to Liam's new wife. But how is that possible? Lynette died in a fiery car wreck years ago.

This one is for Uncle Norb and Aunt Ginny. I love being part of your family. Thanks for all the support and encouragement and my best to you both always.

Prologue

The blur of red taillights on the highway ahead suddenly disappeared in the pouring rain and blackness.

Rozalyn Sawyer hit her brakes, shocked to realize she didn't know where she was. The road didn't look familiar. But it was hard to tell in this part of Oregon with an impenetrable jungle of green just off the pavement.

She'd been following the vehicle ahead of her for the past twenty miles. She'd picked it up outside of Oakridge, happy to see another car on this lonely stretch of highway tonight, especially at this time of year.

In her headlights she'd seen the solitary driver silhouetted behind the wheel of the pickup and felt an odd kinship. Between the rain, the darkness and the isolation, she'd been a little uneasy. But then she'd been feeling that way ever since she'd heard her father hadn't returned from his recent camping trip.

She vaguely remembered seeing a detour sign in the middle of the highway just before the pickup had turned. She'd followed the truck in front of her as the driver turned on to the narrower road to the left, and didn't remember any other roads off of this one.

But now she saw that the pavement ended. With a shock she realized where she was. Lost Creek Falls. She felt shaken, confused. How had she ended up on the dead-end road to the waterfall?

She'd been following the red taillights in front of her and not paying attention, that's how. The driver must have taken a wrong turn back at the detour sign and she'd blindly followed him. She'd been distracted, worrying about her father. As far as she could tell, no one had seen or heard from him in more than two weeks—and that included Emily, his bride of six months.

"I told you. He took his truck and camper and his camera, just like he always does," Emily had said when Roz called her yesterday. "He said he'd be back when he came back and not to concern myself. He was very clear about that."

Yes, for a few days. Not for two weeks. Liam Sawyer was in great shape for his age. He would be sixty on Thanksgiving Day, but Roz worried he might be trying to act even younger after marrying a woman fifteen years his junior.

Since no one had heard from him, Roz was sick with worry that something had happened. And now this "detour" would only make her arrival in Timber Falls all that much later.

The other driver had turned around in the gravel parking lot and stopped, his headlights blinding her as she pulled past and started to turn around.

The moonless rainy darkness and the dense forest

closed in around her car as she began her turn. Remote areas like this had always unnerved her, especially since from the time she was a child she'd known what was really out there.

Suddenly someone ran through her headlights. All she caught was a flash of yellow raincoat. She hit her brakes and stared ahead of her as the person wearing the bright yellow hooded raincoat climbed over the safety barrier at the top of the falls and disappeared in the trees that grew out over the water.

The driver of the pickup? Why would he venture out to the falls on a night like this, she wondered, watching to see if he reappeared.

Suddenly, she spotted the yellow raincoat through the trees at the edge of the falls. The figure seemed to be teetering on the precipice above the roaring water as if—

"Oh, God, no." Roz threw open her door and ran coatless through the icy cold rain toward the waterfall, fear crushing her chest making it nearly impossible to breathe. Not again. Dear God, not again.

"Don't!" she cried, still a dozen yards away.

The person didn't look her way, didn't even acknowledge hearing her. Through the rain and darkness, Roz ran, watching in horror as the bright yellow raincoat seemed to waver before it fell forward, dropping over the edge, and being instantly swallowed up in the spray of the falls.

Roz raced to the railing but couldn't see anything past the trees. Panicked, she ran around the barrier and pushed her way through the tree limbs, praying she'd find the person clinging to the edge.

The roar of the waterfall was deafening. She could feel the spray, warmer than the rain falling around her as she worked her way out onto the moss-slick boulders. She'd had a horrible fear of heights for the past ten years.

But her fear for the jumper was stronger than for herself as she grasped the slim branch of a pine tree leaning out over the waterfall.

Holding on fiercely, she stepped to the edge, her heart dropping as she glimpsed something bright yellow churning in the dark waters below.

She let out a cry and tried to step back. The limb in her hand broke and suddenly she was trying to find purchase on the wet, slick moss at her feet.

With the roar of the waterfall in her ears, she didn't hear him. Nor did she realize he'd come out onto the rocks above the dizzying dark water until he grabbed her from behind.

Chapter One

It was late when Charity Jenkins heard someone come in to the *Timber Falls Courier* newspaper office, and realized she'd forgotten to lock the front door.

Her hand dropped to the desk drawer and the Derringer she now kept there. She'd put it in the desk after almost being killed a few weeks before. Unfortunately, as the days had gone by, she'd become lax again about security. Probably because for almost thirty years, she'd been safe in Timber Falls.

"Dammit, Charity, if you're going to work late, you've got to lock the door," Sheriff Mitch Tanner barked as he came through the dark doorway.

She let out the breath she'd been holding and gently lowered the gun back into the drawer. "Forgot." She smiled up at him as he moved in to the pool of light at her desk. Her heart did a little dippy-do-da dance, as it always did at the sight of him.

He was tall and dark with two perfect deep-set dimples, a Tanner trait. Gorgeous and impossible and the only man for her.

She watched him glance around the small newspaper office. As owner, publisher, editor and reporter, she often worked late. Her only help was a high school student who came in some evenings. This wasn't one of those evenings.

So it was just the two of them. Which was nice since it had been a few days since she'd seen the good sheriff.

For years she'd been trying to get him to realize he couldn't live without her. True, there'd been moments when he'd weakened and kissed her. But he'd always taken off like a shot, holding fast to his conviction that he wasn't good marriage material and that the two of them together would be murder.

That is, until recently. A few weeks ago, after she'd almost been killed, Mitch had asked her out. On a real date. It had been nothing short of miraculous. Same with the date. And there'd been more kissing. He'd even given her a silver bracelet she'd once admired. The entire episode had bowled her over completely. Maybe there was hope after all.

Unfortunately, she could tell that he was still fighting the inevitable as if he thought there was some doubt that they'd be getting married. Obviously, he didn't believe, like Charity did, that love conquered all.

"You're working late," he said, coming around to pull up a chair next to her desk. His gaze went to the open drawer and her gun. With a groan, he reached over to close the drawer. "Tell me it isn't loaded."

"What would be the point of an unloaded gun?" she asked, wondering why he'd stopped by.

"Try not to shoot yourself, okay?"

She grinned at him. Just the sight of him made her day. Maybe he was here to ask her to that dance at the community center this coming weekend. Or maybe he'd just come by for a kiss. Her lips tingled expectantly at the thought.

But that hope was quickly dashed when he pushed back his sheriff's hat and put on his official business face.

He cleared his throat and said, "You're going to hear about this anyway so I thought the best thing to do—"

"What is it?" she asked, sitting up a little straighter. He'd come to tell her something he didn't want to tell her. This ought to be good. Almost as good as a kiss. Almost.

"You were right," he said, the words clearly difficult for him.

She sat back. Oh yeah, this day just couldn't get any better. "I'm sorry. I don't think I heard you correctly?"

"You heard me. You were right. The shot that killed Bud Farnsworth didn't come from Daisy Dennison's gun. It came from Wade's."

Charity jerked back in her chair, the ramifications of his words nearly flooring her. "I knew it. I told you Wade Dennison was in on the kidnapping!"

Wade Dennison was the owner of Dennison Ducks, the local decoy factory outside of town and the largest employer in Timber Falls. Wade had shocked the town by bringing home a much younger wife thirty years ago.

They had a daughter right away, Desiree. Then two years later another one, Angela. Several weeks after Angela's birth the baby disappeared from her crib never to be seen again. There'd been rumors that the baby wasn't Wade's.

No ransom demand was ever made. No body ever found. Daisy Dennison, who'd been the talk of the town, became a recluse after her youngest daughter's disappearance. That is until Halloween, when she'd showed up with a gun at the Dennison Ducks factory and helped save Charity's life when the decoy foreman had tried to kill them both.

Bud Farnsworth had abducted Charity to retrieve a letter that implicated him in Angela Dennison's disappearance. A Dennison Ducks employee named Nina Monroe had mailed the letter to the *Timber Falls Courier,* Charity's newspaper, right before she was killed. Nina had more than a few secrets, it turned out, and a flair for blackmail.

Bud destroyed the letter before anyone could read it—including Charity much to her regret—but there was no doubt now that he was somehow involved in kidnapping the baby.

The only question that had remained was: Did he act alone?

Charity was sure he didn't. In fact, she was damned sure that Wade Dennison had hired Bud to get rid of the baby because he believed Angela wasn't his. Just before Bud died, he'd tried to talk and he'd been looking right at Wade at the time.

Charity was convinced that Wade had shot Bud to shut him up, and now that she knew Wade had fired the fatal shot that killed Bud—and not his wife, Daisy—Charity was even more convinced of Wade's guilt.

"Wade *was* behind the kidnapping," Charity said. "This is exactly why I wanted to tell you about this myself."

She rolled her eyes. "You told me because you knew I was going to find out." And here she'd been hoping he'd come by just to see her.

"Maybe I thought I could keep you from doing a story that might get you killed."

"You romantic, you."

"I'm serious, Charity. I'm worried about you and what you're going to do next."

"Mitch, I saw Bud try to say something to Wade right before he died," Charity said, feeling a chill at the memory. "He was going to incriminate Wade. That's why Wade shot him, so the truth would never come out."

"We don't know that for a fact and speculating only leads to trouble. Especially in print. I would have thought you'd have learned that by now."

She smiled. This was an old argument between them. "I'm a newspaper woman. It's my job to get to the truth, and sometimes I have to rattle a few cages to do that and you wouldn't be worried unless you thought I was right about Wade Dennison being a dangerous man."

Mitch took off his hat and raked his fingers through his hair. "Is there any way I can talk you out of this?"

She cocked her head at him. "What did you have

in mind?'' And to think not long ago she'd thought, if she could just write a Pulitzer Prize-winning story, Mitch would finally realize he couldn't live without her and ask her to marry him.

Instead, she'd realized that Mitch would have been happier if she wasn't a journalist at all. For some reason, he worried about her safety. Maybe because a lot of her stories got her into trouble.

He put his hat back on—and his official face.

She could play that game, too. ''Have you talked to Wade?'' she asked, knowing there was no way Wade was going to speak to her on the record or off.

''He admits he could have fired the fatal shot but says all he could think about was saving his wife, Daisy. That's the official statement.'' Mitch reached in to his coat and brought out a folded sheet of paper. He handed it to her.

''I figured that would be his story,'' she said, unfolding the paper to see that it was an official statement from the sheriff's office. She tossed it aside. ''I'll be careful what I print, but Mitch, what if I'm right?''

His dark eyes settled on her. ''If you're right, then Wade Dennison is a killer. You might want to keep that in mind.''

''But how do we prove it?'' she cried. ''We can't let him get away with murder.''

''*We* aren't going to prove it,'' he said getting to his feet. ''I am. I have no intention of letting him get away with murder—if he's guilty. But Charity, as hard as this is for you, you might be wrong this time.''

She smirked at that. "You know I'm right ninety-nine percent of the time."

He shook his head but seemed unable not to smile down at her. "You *are* something."

A person could take that a number of ways.

"Try to accept the fact that we may never know what happened to Angela Dennison," he said after a moment.

She couldn't stand the thought. "There has to be a way."

Mitch was shaking his head. "Charity, getting involved last time almost cost you your life."

True. But it had also made Mitch realize that he cared for her. She wisely didn't point this out to him though.

He stood looking down at her as if there was more he wanted to say. She waited for him to ask her to the dance. Or maybe to a late dinner. It had been almost a week since he'd kissed her.

"Just be careful, okay?" he said quietly.

She smiled up at him. "You know me."

"Yeah, that's what worries me." He turned to leave. "See you later." She hoped so as she watched him go, her lips feeling neglected.

She got up and locked the front door as he drove away. Then she turned back to her computer. She had a story to write.

The phone rang. She picked it up, already knowing who it would be.

"I got that ballistics report you wanted," said her source on the other end of the line. "Are you sitting down?"

She sat, even though she already knew the results. "Wade Dennison's gun killed Bud Farnsworth."

"You're the best, Tommy." A thought had been percolating ever since Mitch left. If she was right and Wade Dennison had hired Bud Farnsworth to do his dirty work, then there would be a money trail. "Tommy, I have another little favor."

"Little?" he cried when he heard what she wanted. "Do you realize how many years in prison I could get for hacking in to bank records?"

"More years than hacking in to the state investigation's office for a ballistics report?" she asked innocently.

He laughed. "What's the name on the account?"

"Two accounts. Wade Dennison and Bud Farnsworth. And I'm interested in old records—say twenty-seven years ago? Let me give you the dates."

Tommy let out a low whistle when she'd finished. "I hope you know what you're doing."

"Are you kidding?" She hung up and typed Wade Dennison Fired Fatal Bullet To Silence Kidnapper or Save Wife? Angela Dennison Kidnapping Still A Mystery and stopped, reminding herself that Wade had threatened her life not that long ago. True, he did it in front of the sheriff—and she hadn't taken it all that seriously. But now…now she wasn't so sure she didn't have something to fear.

Not that it would stop her from doing the story. Or doing a little checking into both Dennison's and Farnsworth's bank accounts. After all, she was a journalist whether Mitch liked it or not and she came from a family of the best gossips in four counties.

She hated not knowing what was really going on. There had to be a way to get to the truth.

The problem was Wade might be the only one left alive who knew the truth about Angela Dennison's kidnapping. Maybe it was possible to make Wade angry enough to do something that would get him caught.

She began to type again, telling herself that Mitch wasn't going to be happy about this. Nothing new about that. Too bad, though, that he hadn't kissed her. She feared that by tomorrow morning when the paper came out, kissing her would be the furthest thing from his mind.

THE ROAR of the waterfall drowned out Roz's scream as she tried to fight off the strong arms that grabbed her from behind.

Frantic, she struggled to regain her balance, to free herself of his hold. As she lost her footing on the wet moss-slick boulder, she felt the earth tilt and all she could see was the dizzying darkness of the water below as she slipped and started to fall toward the gorge.

The arms around her loosened as if he realized he was going to pitch over the waterfall with her if he didn't let go with one arm and try to grab something to save himself.

She drove her elbow into his ribs and heard him let out an oath, but he held on and suddenly she was jerked backward. He took her down with him, both of them hitting hard as they fell under the wide base of a pine tree a few feet from the edge of the falls.

"Stay away from me," she cried, scooting back

from him as her hands searched for something to defend herself with. Her fingers closed around a chunk of wet wood. She held it up, brandishing the wood like a club, as she struggled to get her feet under her.

It was dark under the tree. Not even the light from her SUV's headlamps could reach it. But she could see that he was large as he also rose to his feet. His face was in a shadow, his features a blur, but his eyes— The irises were so pale they seemed almost iridescent in the dim light.

He advanced on her, his hands out as if in surrender, but she knew he was just looking for another opening to lunge for her again.

"You come near me and I'll hit you," she yelled over the roar of the waterfall as she backed up as far as she could. "I'm warning you."

"Fine," he said and stopped. "Go ahead, jump. I don't care. My mistake for trying to save you from yourself."

She blinked at him through the mist and rain. "Save me from myself? I wasn't going to *jump*."

"Right. Whatever. Go ahead. Have at it. Believe me, I won't try to stop you again." He crossed his arms over his chest. She noticed for the first time that, like her, he wasn't wearing a coat. His shirt and slacks were soaked. Just as hers were.

"You weren't trying to push me off the waterfall?"

He glared at her. "Are you crazy? What am I saying? Of course you're crazy or you wouldn't be up here in the middle of a damned rainstorm trying to commit suicide. And this is the thanks I get for attempting to save your life."

"Thanks? You almost killed us both," she snapped. "And I told you, I wasn't trying to kill myself." She shuddered at the thought.

"Uh-huh. You just wanted to get a good look at the waterfall." He started to turn away. "Well, have a good look. I won't bother you anymore."

"I saw someone jump."

He stopped and turned slowly. "What?"

"I saw someone in a yellow raincoat jump." She glanced off to the side toward the waterfall, sick with the memory. "That's why I rushed over here."

"You saw someone?"

Could his tone be any more mocking?

"I think it was a woman." Had she caught a glimpse of long blond hair just before the figure disappeared over the top of the falls? "I saw her—" her voice broke "—lean forward and drop over the edge. When I got to the top of the falls, the yellow raincoat she was wearing was in the water below."

"Uh-huh," he said and looked around. "And this woman who jumped, where is her car?"

"Right over—"

"That's my truck. But you ought to know that. You've been following me for the past twenty miles."

She looked past her own car, the engine still running, the interior light on since she'd left her door open in her haste. The headlights sliced a narrow swath of pale gold through the pouring rain and darkness. There were no other vehicles. Just hers. And his. Nor had she seen any other cars on the highway tonight.

"How did this mysterious jumper get out here?" he asked.

She shook her head, confused. The waterfall was too far from anything for anyone to have walked. Especially this time of year in a rainstorm.

"You and I are the only ones out here," he said.

She opened her mouth, then closed it. She'd seen someone in a bright yellow raincoat, seen the person jump, seen the coat in the water below the falls.

Even back here under the shelter of the large old pine, she could still feel that falling sensation, the roaring in her ears, the warm spray on her face, feel the watery grave far, far below as her feet slipped on the mossy rock.

"You had to have seen her," Roz said trembling hard now but not from the cold.

"All I saw was you in my side mirror as I started to leave. I saw you throw on your brakes, bolt from your car and run to the edge of the waterfall."

He'd been watching *her?* That's why he hadn't seen the person in the yellow raincoat. So he'd just been trying to save her? "If I was wrong about your intentions—"

He waved off her apology. "Forget it."

"We have to call the sheriff." Even as she said it, she knew no one could have survived that fall into the rocks and water below. It would just be a matter of recovering the body.

"You have a cell phone that works up here?" he asked. "I tried mine when I stopped. No service."

She shook her head. Of course there wouldn't be

any service up here. "I'll call the sheriff when I get closer to Timber Falls."

"You sure you want to do that?"

She rubbed a hand over her wet face, still holding the chunk of wood in the other. She was exhausted, emotionally drained. She leveled her gaze at him. "I *did* see someone jump." She didn't know where the person had come from but she knew what she'd seen.

He shrugged. "Whatever you say."

She hated his scornful tone. Had he really been trying to save her? Or kill her? If he'd just left her alone, she would have been perfectly fine. She was pretty sure that was true. He was making her doubt everything.

"I have family in Timber Falls," she said, and hated herself for trying to reassure him that she was the sane one here. "I'm on my way there."

"If your family lives in Timber Falls, I'd think you would know the road."

"I wasn't paying attention. I was following *you*. And I haven't been up here in years." She wouldn't be here at all if she wasn't worried about her father. When she'd left ten years before, she'd thought nothing could ever get her back to Timber Falls. And nothing had, not even when her father had remarried, moved back and reopened her childhood home. Until now. "I came up here tonight because—"

"Thanks, but I'd prefer not to know anymore about you," he said.

"Are you always this disagreeable?" she snapped.

"Actually, I'm trying to be on my best behavior right now."

"Really?"

"Really," he said, wringing the water from his shirttail. "You should see me when I'm not."

"No, thanks."

"Did I mention that I'm late for a dinner engagement?"

"Then please don't let me keep you," she said.

He started backing away from her. "And please don't thank me for saving your life. Really."

"No problem. I hadn't wanted to jump but now that I've met you I might change my mind."

His laugh held little humor as he turned his back on her and stalked through the rain toward the parking lot and his pickup.

She headed for her car, still gripping the chunk of wood just in case he was a psycho killer and planned to double back. He didn't. He went straight to his pickup, climbed in and a moment later the engine turned over and the headlights came on. He drove away without looking back as far as she could tell.

Her driver's-side seat was soaked and so was she. Not that she wasn't already chilled to the bone from everything that had happened.

She locked her car door, feeling scared and not sure why as she kicked up the heat. There was no other vehicle. Maybe the person who'd jumped from the waterfall had hidden her car somewhere. But why do that?

As Roz pulled out of the parking lot, tears stung her eyes. She hadn't imagined the person in the yellow raincoat. And history was not repeating itself.

Chapter Two

Rain pounded the windshield, the wipers making a steady *whap-whap* as Roz drove the narrow road back out to the main highway. She didn't see the pickup's taillights. He obviously didn't want her following him anymore and had sped off to avoid any further contact. Fine with her.

Stopping at the intersection, she looked through the rain for the detour sign she vaguely remembered seeing earlier.

It was gone.

Had he picked it up? He hadn't seen the person in the yellow raincoat. Was it possible he hadn't seen the detour sign, either? She shook off the thought. Why had he turned down the road to the waterfall then?

She hit the gas, even more anxious to get to Timber Falls. The night seemed too dark, too rainy, too isolated. She couldn't wait to see the lights of town, to get to the house, to see that her father had returned so that all her worry had been for nothing.

The rainforest grew in a dark, wet canopy over the top of the narrow, winding highway. Rain splattered down through the vegetation, striking the windshield like pebbles as mist rose ghostlike up from the pavement.

A few miles down the highway, the trees opened a little, and she dug out her cell phone, saw that she had service and called 9-1-1. She related briefly what she'd seen at Lost Creek Falls to the dispatcher and left her cell phone number for the sheriff to call her back.

When the lights of Timber Falls appeared out of the rain and mist, Roz felt such a surge of relief she almost wept. Home—the feeling surprised her given why she'd left here. This hadn't been home for ten years. Nor would it ever be again. But right now, she was overjoyed to finally be here, the one place she'd once felt safe and happy.

She drove down Main Street past the city offices, the Duck Inn bar, the *Timber Falls Courier* and the Busy Bee. The No Vacancy sign glowed red at the Ho Hum Motel and Betty's Café was packed, a half dozen cars parked out front. That was odd. She frowned, wondering why everything was so busy given the time of year—and the weather. Something must be going on.

As she turned down the once familiar tree-lined lane, she felt as if time had stood still here as well. Anxiously she awaited her first glimpse of the large old house where she'd been raised.

She'd never understood why her father had hung on to the house given the painful memories. He alone had come here over the years, paying to see that the empty house didn't fall into disrepair.

But as the structure came into view in her head-lights, she was overwhelmed with emotion and thank-ful that he hadn't been able to part with it. The house stood fighting back the rainforest, the towering roof-line etched black against the night sky. She caught her breath at the sight of it. As a child she thought it a castle. Even now it seemed larger than life.

This had been home for her first seventeen years. It had been a fun, rambling place with lots of space to play and great hiding places. Her mother always had flowers growing in large pots on the porch and brightly colored curtains at the windows.

But Roz saw that the pots of flowers were gone—just as the brightly colored curtains were, just as her mother was.

Roz looked away, fighting the same sorrow she had for the past ten years, and hoped to see her father's truck and camper parked next to the other cars in the open carport beside the house.

There were three cars. The new Cadillac her father had bought Emily as a wedding present and two new sports cars, a bright yellow one and a shiny black one. The yellow one belonged to Emily's twenty-four-year-old daughter, Suzanne, the black one to her twenty-six-year-old son, Drew.

Roz felt a sliver of apprehension to see that the whole family was here. Her father obviously hadn't returned. Was that what had brought Suzanne and Drew all the way in from Portland? Had something happened since Roz had talked to Emily?

Even more worried, Roz parked in front of the house and made a run through the rain to the porch.

She stood waiting for her father's new family to answer the bell. It felt so strange not to be able to just open the door and walk in. But the people who lived here now were virtual strangers. She'd only been around the new family on a few awkward occasions. Even her father had become a stranger the last six months since his quickie marriage in Las Vegas.

"Give Emily a chance," her dad had asked after the wedding. "I know this happened pretty fast." She should say so! "But please try. For me."

And she was trying. Really.

She rang the bell and managed a smile, relieved to see the door opened by her newly acquired stepbrother Drew, the least objectionable member of her father's new family.

"Hey, you made it. I was starting to worry about you," he said, flashing her a big smile. Drew was blond, blue-eyed and drop-dead handsome if you went for that type. Roz didn't. She found his classically featured face devoid of character with no sign that he'd experienced life, although he was only two years her junior.

Drew's saving grace was the fact that he was the only member of his family who seemed to care one way or another about her. His interest in her definitely wasn't romantic. Roz suspected he paid attention to her because it annoyed his mother.

He hugged Roz, then stepped back in surprise. "You're freezing." He ushered her inside out of the cold and dampness. "What happened?"

She knew she must look like a drowned cocker spaniel, her strawberry-blond hair a tousle of damp curls. "I had a...flat." She really didn't want to get into her "detour" or what she'd seen at the waterfall.

"Has anyone heard from my father?" she asked as she stepped in.

Drew shook his head. "Sorry."

She glanced past him, trying hard not to cry. She hadn't realized how scared she was, how worried that something had happened to him. If only she hadn't missed his call the other day.

What little of the house she could see had changed more than she could have imagined. When Roz's mother, Anna, had been alive, the house had smelled of baked bread and brownies. This house smelled of cleaner, new carpet and fresh paint.

Her father had warned her a few months ago that Emily was doing a little redecorating, but it still came as a shock to see everything of her mother gone. Through the French doors, she could see the living room. All of the beautiful old things her mother had collected had been replaced with new, modern furniture.

That wasn't the only shock. While Roz's mother, Anna, had loved vibrant colors, it seemed Emily was partial to indistinguishable shades of off-white. The furnishings didn't fit the house any more than Emily did, she thought uncharitably.

"Don't worry, all of your mother's things have been moved up to the attic," Drew said, following her gaze. "Your father insisted everything be saved."

The attic. How appropriate.

Emily came breezing out of the dining room looking harried. "Rozalyn," the woman gushed, rushing over to give her a quick air kiss.

Emily Lane Sawyer was blond with blue eyes like her two grown children. She was a tall, statuesque woman, far different from Roz's mother, who'd been petite with soft brown eyes and strawberry-blond hair that curled in the humidity just like her daughter's. Everyone had always said Roz was the spitting image of her mother, something that Emily had remarked on more than one occasion.

In her late forties, Emily was a good fifteen years younger than her new husband. Intellectually, Roz could understand what her father had seen in the woman. She had a great body for her age and she was quite attractive.

What worried Roz was what Emily had seen in Liam Sawyer.

"You made it in time for dinner," Emily said.

Roz heard the "just barely" in her tone. Dinner was the last thing Roz wanted but it would be rude to try to get out of dining with the family. "Drew says you haven't heard from my father." She couldn't bring herself to call him dad with these people.

"No, but like I told you on the phone, Liam said he didn't know when he'd be back and not to worry about him. I hope that isn't the only reason you drove all the way up here."

What other reason than to see her father? "It isn't like him to be gone this long without any word," Roz said, not mentioning the other reason she was so concerned. The strange message on her answering machine. He'd sounded upset, said little, asking her to call as soon as possible.

That had been two days ago. Emily said she hadn't heard from Liam for more than two weeks.

Also he'd left his cell phone number. Not the number at the house. And when Roz had tried to reach him she'd gotten the message that the phone was either out of the calling area or turned off.

He'd said it was important but it had been his tone that scared her. Something had happened, and it had to be something big for her father, the most laid-back man alive, to sound that upset.

And yet no one in this family seemed even concerned about him. Why was that? Because they didn't want her to know that something had happened before he'd left on his latest camping trip. And Roz was certain it had something to do with Emily.

"He's always checked in after a few days," Roz said now. "It's hard to believe you haven't heard from him."

"Well, you know him better than I do," Emily said distractedly. "I have to admit, I don't understand his need to go off into the mountains like he does at his age."

"He loves the Cascades. I'm sure that's one reason he moved back here with you." Actually, it was a mystery why her dad had done something that ridiculous, bringing this woman to Timber Falls. Roz figured there was a lot about Liam that a woman like Emily wouldn't be able to understand. Could her father have picked a woman any more different from him?

"Drew, would you see what is keeping your sister?" Emily said, glancing past Roz. "Our dinner guest will be arriving soon.".

Dinner guest? Roz knew her shock must have shown. Emily wasn't letting any concern over Liam keep her from entertaining, it seemed.

Drew buzzed his sister on the intercom near the front door. "No answer," he said to his mother.

"Has anyone looked for my father?" Roz asked.

Emily seemed surprised by the question. "We wouldn't even know where to look. It would be like searching for a needle in a haystack." She glanced at her watch, obviously more worried about her dinner than her husband, then up at Roz again. "You said yourself he's always done this, gone off alone, no matter the weather, taking his camera and camper back into the mountains, out searching for Bigfoot like everyone else in this town right now. I can't see this time is any different except this time there was an actual sighting."

"There's been a sighting?" That explained the large number of people in town this time of year.

"Two weeks ago. I thought you would have heard," Emily said. "Some fool bread man claimed he saw Bigfoot just outside of town and your father took off like a shot."

Was it possible her father was on the trail of Bigfoot and that's why he hadn't come back? Why he'd sounded the way he had on the phone message? Except he hadn't sounded excited. He'd sounded… upset, almost scared. And he'd been gone way too long.

"I'm afraid he's hurt, trapped somewhere, unable to get out for help," Roz said. "I think we should contact the sheriff."

Emily touched her temple and winced as if she suddenly had a headache. "He's *your* father. Whatever you think is best. I just feel it's a little premature to be calling in the sheriff."

"I don't," Roz said.

Emily sighed. "Drew, darling, would you get my medicine. It's in my purse." She looked past Roz and groaned. "Oh, where is he off to now? He's never around when I need him." She rubbed her temples. "I must see to dinner. By the way, a friend of your father's is joining us. I thought you'd like that."

Roz felt a stab of guilt for her earlier uncharitable thoughts about Emily. "That was very kind of you. Maybe he'll have some idea where my father has gone."

Emily checked her watch again.

"Emily, why do I feel as if there is something you aren't telling me?"

The older woman blinked blank blue eyes at her.

"Did you and Dad have a fight before he left?"

"Of course not." Emily brought herself up to her full height. "I really need to see to my dinner."

Roz sighed. She could hear at least two of her staff in the kitchen doing the actual cooking. It was obvious Emily just wanted to get away. But Roz was sorry she'd brought up the subject now. "So who is this friend of my father's who's coming to dinner?"

"It's a surprise. You really should get into some

dry clothing before you catch your death. You can have a drink before dinner with Suzanne.''

Roz would rather catch her death than have a drink with Drew's sister who was probably half-sloshed by now.

As Emily headed toward the kitchen, Roz heard the front door open behind her and turned to find Drew standing in the foyer. He had her suitcase in one hand, her camera bag in the other. She hadn't heard him leave.

''It finally stopped raining but I've heard there's another storm on the way. I brought your things in,'' he said, studying her openly as if concerned about her conversation with his mother.

''Thank you.'' She appreciated his thoughtfulness more than he could know.

''Where's Mother?'' he asked.

''She's seeing to dinner. She said she invited a friend of my father's to join us.'' Drew seemed surprised. ''I'm hoping he might know where my father went. I know your mother isn't concerned—''

''Mother hides her feelings,'' he said as he started for the stairs. ''She was just telling me earlier that she wished Liam had shown up before your visit. She's much more worried than she's letting on.''

Sure she was.

When Roz didn't comment, he said in an obvious attempt to change the subject, ''Planning to do some shooting while you're here?''

''I never go anywhere without my camera.''

''You must have gotten that from your dad,'' Drew said. ''Except he says for him it's just a hobby and he could never be as good as you. Your photographs really are amazing. I saw your latest book. It's your best yet.''

''Thank you.'' She was surprised he even knew she had a new photography book out but if he was trying to flatter her, he was succeeding quite well.

''Mother had the maid get your old room ready,'' he said over his shoulder.

She barely heard him. ''Were you here when my father left?'' she asked, still convinced Emily wasn't telling her something. Something important.

''I guess I was.''

Was it just her imagination that his back stiffened at her question? Her dad had told her that Drew had moved in after getting a new job so he could work from Timber Falls via computer and help his mother with the house remodeling.

''Did my father seem…upset? Or act differently?''

''Not that I noticed.'' He reached the second floor landing and continued on up to the third floor without turning to look back at her.

Roz stared after him, more convinced than ever that something had happened before her father's departure. Something Drew and his mother were keeping from her.

As Roz passed the second floor, she heard a voice she recognized. Drew's sister, Suzanne, had a distinct whine that was easily recognizable even from a distance. She must be on the phone. Roz wondered why Suzanne hadn't answered the intercom when Drew had buzzed her.

As Roz hurried up the stairs after Drew, she

couldn't help but remember the happy times in this house. She and her best friend, Charity, used to pretend that each room was a separate house in town where they lived happily ever after with their husbands and children and neighbors. She smiled ruefully at the memory of this house ringing with their laughter. She and Charity had both thought that one day their own children would race along these worn wooden floors as they had done.

She pushed the thought away as she and Drew reached the third floor.

"Mother hasn't gotten this far yet in her remodel," Drew said.

Roz swallowed hard as she looked down the hallway. This floor looked exactly as it had ten years ago. Her room had always been on the third floor just down from her mother's sewing room and her father's studio and darkroom. When she was young, they would put her to bed, then her mother would sew, her father would work in his darkroom. They had wanted her close by.

Her parents' bedroom had been on the second floor along with several guest rooms. Her mother had installed an intercom so she could always be within earshot of her daughter.

It was crazy, but for a moment, Roz thought she heard her mother's favorite song playing on the old phonograph in the sewing room. If she listened hard, she thought she would hear her father whistling a little off key in his darkroom down the hall. But hadn't he told her that Emily was doing away with the darkroom because she'd purchased him a digital camera?

Drew stopped in front of Roz's former bedroom door and waited for her. "Don't look so worried. Your room is exactly as you left it. Liam insisted."

Her feet felt like leaded weights as she walked down the hall to slowly turn the knob.

As the door swung open, Roz caught a glimpse of the whimsical quilt her mother had spent months stitching in secret for her thirteenth birthday. It was still on the bed, just where she'd left it. Albert, the stuffed teddy bear she'd loved threadbare, sat in the corner still wearing the tuxedo her mother had made for the tea parties she and Charity always had at the brightly painted table and chairs. On the table was the little tin tray her mother served the tiny chocolate chip cookies she'd made for them.

Roz swallowed, fighting the stinging tears that burned her eyes and choked off her throat. Drew was right. Her room was exactly as she'd left it ten years ago after her mother's death. Everywhere she looked in this room she saw her mother.

"Roz, are you all right?"

The room magnified her loss. Forcing her back to those horrible days after her mother's death. She couldn't face the loss any more now than she could at seventeen.

"Roz?"

"I'm fine," she said, realizing it wasn't near the truth. She could feel Drew's gaze on her. She glanced over at him, ready to reassure him. What she saw in his expression stopped her.

"Hey, maybe you'd better sit down," he said putting down her suitcase and camera bag to take her arm and lead her over to the wicker chair by the window.

Had she only imagined that he'd seemed to be enjoying her discomfort at seeing this room? He looked and sounded concerned *now*. She told herself she was tired. Imagining things. Like she'd imagined someone in a yellow raincoat leaping into Lost Creek Falls?

"I'm fine. Really," she said to Drew, watching him for some sign of the expression she'd thought she'd seen only moments before. "I just need to get out of these damp clothes."

He backed toward the door, still studying her openly. "I know how hard this must be for you. Come on down soon for a drink before dinner. You look like you could use one."

She nodded and tried to smile.

"Mother went all out on dinner tonight."

"Do you know who the guest is?" she asked, getting to her feet to see Drew out. She needed some time alone. Pretending she was all right was exhausting.

"It's a surprise." He shrugged as if to say, "You know Mother."

Except she didn't know Emily. She suspected though that the woman was big on surprises. She'd certainly surprised Roz by somehow getting Liam to marry her.

"Buzz me on the intercom if you need *anything*. Two buzzes, okay?"

She nodded. "Thanks." Closing the door behind him, she turned to look at the room again, fighting tears of grief and worry and anger. How could her father bring his new wife back to this house? This house so filled with memories of Roz's mother? The room seemed to echo all the unanswered questions Roz had been asking herself for the past ten years.

First her mother and now there was the chance that her father—

She brushed at her tears, refusing to let herself even think that she might lose him, too. Cold, her clothing still damp, she went to the large antique bureau. In the third drawer she found what she'd been looking for. The thick rust-colored sweater her mother had knitted for her. It was the last thing her mother had made her. The sweater still fit.

She pulled on a pair of jeans from her suitcase and hiking boots, needing to get out of the house for a few minutes. She took the back stairs, exiting through a door that opened into her mother's garden.

The night felt cold and damp but for the moment the rain had stopped. Only the faint tingle of electricity in the air foretold of an approaching storm. She took a deep breath and let it out slowly as she started down the stone path to the rear of the property.

Like the house, her father had seen that the garden had been maintained. But in this part of the country, it was a constant battle to hold back the rainforest and no one had a way with plants like Anna Sawyer had. Roz could see where there had been recent digging. Emily must have hired someone to redo the garden as well as the house.

Roz walked down the winding overgrown path as far as the rock arch where a tangle of vines and tree limbs had left only a narrow opening. Quiet settled over her as she stood in the shadowed darkness. From here she could barely see the house through the trees and vines.

She no longer felt like crying, which was good. She needed to be strong now—for her father. She felt like she was the only person here who was worried about him.

"What does that tell you?" she asked the night as she looked back at the house. "I can't understand how you could have gotten involved with someone like her." A younger, good-looking woman? "Okay, maybe I can understand the attraction—at first. You were lonely." The thought broke her heart. "Of course you were lonely. But something happened, didn't it?" She knew her father. He wouldn't just stay away like this. He'd called her the night before last and hadn't tried to get back to her. "What happened? What was it you needed to talk to me about?"

A breeze stirred the tops of the trees in a low moan. She took another deep breath and looked up at the night sky as if it held all the answers. Clouds skimmed over the faint glitter of distant stars. No moon. She tried to fight back her growing panic. Her every instinct told her that her father needed her, and it was imperative that she find him. Was it too much to hope that this mystery dinner guest and friend of her father's might know something?

Mist rose from the wet ground around her. She hugged herself against the dampness, not ready to go back inside. Not yet. She took another deep breath, the air scented with cedar and rainwater and damp fertile earth, and so wonderfully familiar except for—

She took another sniff. A chill skittered across her bare arms. Her heart began to knock as she picked up a scent that didn't belong on the night breeze—and, eyes adjusting to the darkness, she saw a large, still shape that didn't belong in the garden.

Someone was hiding just inches from her on the other side of the rock arch.

Chapter Three

"Wait!" Ford reached for her, hoping to stop her before she panicked and did something crazy. Like scream bloody murder. Too late. She got out one startled cry as she stumbled back from him, then she let out a bloodcurdling shriek that he knew could be heard in three counties.

He cursed himself for not warning her he was out here. At first he hadn't wanted to scare her. Once he recognized her voice, he wasn't about to open his mouth. What the hell was she doing here, anyway?

He caught her arm and spun her around, figuring once she recognized him she'd at least quit screaming. But her eyes were squeezed tightly shut, her mouth open, a shriek coming out.

Behind them, twenty yards away through the trees, the back porch light blinked on. Any moment the lady of the house would be calling the sheriff and—

He did the first thing that came to mind short of throttling the woman. When she took a breath, he kissed her, covering any future screams as his mouth dropped to hers. She gasped in surprise, eyes fluttering open for an instant, then shuttering closed again.

She had a great mouth, and for a few seconds, he got lost in her lush lips, in the warmth of her breath mingling with his, in the taste of her.

For those few seconds, he forgot whom he was kissing. He loosened his hold on her as the kiss deepened.

The right hook came out of nowhere. He managed to duck that one. But he hadn't been expecting the kick. Her boot connected with his shin.

"Damn." *He* should have been the one screaming.

She turned to run, mouth open, ready to let out another shriek. He grabbed her around the waist, dragged her back to his chest and clamped a hand over her mouth.

They were both breathing hard now, hidden in the dark shadows of the trees out of sight of whoever was now on the porch calling, "Rozalyn?"

"Listen," he whispered next to her ear. "I didn't mean to scare you."

She tried to slug him again in answer.

"I'm just trying to get to dinner, dammit," he whispered in exasperation.

THE INSTANT his words registered, Roz stopped struggling and groaned. She could hear Emily calling her name, and saw through the tree limbs the dim glow of the porch light in the distance. This man in the dark was no crazed killer hiding in the backyard. Just the dinner guest. She kicked herself mentally and wished the ground would open up and swallow her whole.

He slowly removed his hand from her mouth, obviously afraid she'd scream again. Behind her, she heard him clear his throat and step back almost as if he were afraid she'd kick him again.

She turned, an apology on the tip of her tongue. It never made it to her lips as she got her first good look at him.

"You?!" she whispered in horror. His face was bathed in the mottled pattern of light coming through the trees from the porch lamp. Her first impression earlier at the waterfall had been true. He was tall, broad-shouldered and dark except for his eyes, which were an eerie, pale blue-green.

He wasn't even handsome. His expression was too severe, brows pinched together, full mouth a grim line between the rough stubble of his designer beard. But he was definitely the man who'd almost killed her at Lost Creek Falls. "You *can't* be the dinner guest."

"Emily *invited* me," he said, obviously also trying to keep his voice down. "Anyway, why can't I?"

"Because you were sneaking in the back way!" she hissed.

"I'm *staying* in the guest house. What other way should I be coming from for dinner?" he whispered back.

"You're staying in the guest house?"

"Emily was kind enough to offer it."

"Emily is *so* thoughtful." Roz couldn't believe her stepmother would let a perfect stranger stay in the guest house. But this man wasn't a perfect stranger— not to her father and maybe not to Emily.

She could not believe her father would befriend

such an obnoxious man. "So when was the last time you saw Liam?" she asked.

"It's been a while. Any chance we could discuss this after dinner? I'm hungry."

"Rozalyn!" Emily called again. "Is that you out there?" She sounded as if she were straining to see into the trees and darkness.

"Answer her," he whispered. "I would, but then she'd think I was the one who was screaming."

"Rozalyn?" Emily's tone had an almost hysterical edge to it.

He gave Roz a pleading look.

She groaned. "Yes, it's me," she called back through the trees and the distance between her and the house.

"Well, why in heaven's name were you screaming?" Emily yelled.

Roz sighed. "There was a big disgusting rat by the stone arch."

"Cute," he whispered.

"Ohhhhhhhh," Emily cried. "Rats? Oh! Please come in. Our guest will be arriving any moment now for dinner. I don't want you scaring him out of his wits."

"Too late for that," he muttered under his breath and narrowed his gaze at her. "You're having dinner, too, I take it?" He didn't sound any happier about that than she was. "So, this must be the family you said you had here."

"This is *not* my family," she snapped.

"Whatever." He glanced toward the house. "But

don't you think we should go in to dinner? Emily is going to wonder what's keeping me if not you.''

Let her wonder, Roz thought. ''Why didn't you say something to let me know you were by the arch?'' What had he overheard? She hated to think.

''I didn't want to interrupt the conversation you were having with yourself. I thought you might lose your train of thought.''

Funny.

''Rozalyn, who are you talking to out there?'' Emily called.

''And the kiss?'' Roz whispered, ignoring Emily. ''What was *that* about?''

''*Nothing.* Absolutely nothing. I just wanted to shut you up before you got the whole household out here.''

Flatterer. She fought the urge to kick him again.

''Are you finished interrogating me?'' he asked quietly. ''I'm going in even if you aren't.'' He stepped past her.

She let him lead the way to the house, not trusting him behind her anyway. While she could think of nothing she wanted to do less than to have dinner with this man, she didn't feel like hiding in the garden all night. And now she was curious as to how Emily knew this man well enough to invite him to stay in the guest house. Especially with her husband gone. Especially since this man was closer to Emily's age than Liam was. Especially since Emily would find him attractive, Roz would just bet on that.

If he was telling the truth and he really was a friend of her father's, she was dying to know how they'd met and what they could possibly have in common.

As she followed him along the winding path through the thick vegetation, she realized she didn't even know his name. Not that she really cared. She'd already found out one important thing about the man: he lied. The kiss was hardly *nothing*.

If he'd lie about a kiss… Who knew what else he'd lied about? And how much of a coincidence was it that the two of them had met at Lost Creek Falls earlier tonight under very strange circumstances only to have him turn up here?

FORD COULDN'T BELIEVE his bad luck. Running into the woman not once tonight but twice. Worse, it seemed Emily had invited her to dinner. He swore under his breath as he neared the house. Why hadn't this Rozalyn gone to her own family for dinner? Whoever she was, she was obviously nuts even if she really hadn't been trying to leap off the waterfall earlier.

She was a looker, too. That wild head of strawberry-blond curls, those big brown eyes and that obviously nicely put together body. Why were the great-looking ones the most cuckoo? And this one was unpredictable to boot.

A deadly combination.

He shook his head at his misfortune. But he could get through one dinner with this bunch. After all, he didn't have much choice if he hoped to accomplish what he'd come here for.

"Rozalyn?" Emily called again.

"We were just coming in," she answered behind him, adding an irritated sigh.

"We?" Emily inquired as he and Rozalyn came into view. "Oh. I see you've met."

"We were just getting acquainted," he said.

"You look like you've been wrestling in the weeds," Emily said, eyeing them both.

Rozalyn plucked a leaf from his hair and smiled at him with a devilish gleam in her eyes. She was actually enjoying ticking off her host.

"Let's go right on into the dining room. The rest are already seated," Emily said, clearly annoyed.

"I hope I didn't hold up dinner," he said. Rozalyn, he noticed, hung back as he mounted the steps of the back porch to Emily.

"Oh, no, you're right on time," Emily said, gracing him with a smile as she took his arm and led him toward the back door. "We're just delighted that you could join us."

"As am I," he said, the tension between the two women like sloughing through neck-deep mud, as Rozalyn followed them inside.

Emily still had hold of his arm as they stepped through a set of French doors into a large dining room.

He thought for a moment that Rozalyn had changed her mind about joining them for dinner, but when he glanced over his shoulder, he saw that she'd stopped in the wide French doorway and was now watching him with obvious suspicion.

"I just realized—"

"I hope you're hungry," Emily said as if Rozalyn hadn't spoken.

"—that I didn't catch your—"

"Starved," he said.

"—name," Rozalyn finished.

"I'd like you to meet my daughter," Emily said. A woman in her late twenties was seated at the round dining room table. She and a young man who resembled her had had their heads together when he and Emily had come in. Now the two looked up in surprise, cutting off an obviously intimate conversation in midsentence and appearing almost…guilty.

"This is my daughter Suzanne and my son Drew," Emily said. "Mr. Lancaster has graciously accepted my invitation to dine with us tonight."

"Lancaster?" Rozalyn said behind him in the doorway.

He turned to look at her and felt himself tense at the frown on her face. Clearly, she was trying to place the name.

Drew, who appeared to be a few years older than his sister, had gotten to his feet and was holding out his hand. Ford took it but noticed the young man's attention was more on Rozalyn.

"Mr. Lancaster is staying in our guest house for a while," Emily was saying.

"Really?" Suzanne was a younger version of her mother. Slim, blond and blue-eyed. Her eyes seemed a little glazed, and he noticed that not only was her dirty wineglass empty, but also the bottle in front of her was almost spent.

"Lancaster?" Rozalyn repeated from the doorway.

"Why don't you sit by my daughter," Emily said to him.

He went around the table, aware that Rozalyn still

hadn't joined them. Emily had left a chair between Suzanne and Drew for her other guest.

"Rozalyn, if you'd care to join us," Emily said, her tone as sharp as a glass shard. "Let's not have a scene in front of Liam's friend and our dinner guest."

Rozalyn didn't seem to hear her. Nor was she looking at the older woman. Instead, her gaze was locked on Ford. "I missed your first name, *Mr. Lancaster*."

He met Rozalyn's brown-eyed gaze, almost afraid to tell her but not sure why. Emily hadn't even raised an eyebrow when he'd told her. "Ford. Ford Lancaster."

"Ford Lancaster?!" Roz spat and stepped toward him as if she planned to leap the table and go for his throat. She definitely looked like she wanted to. "You lying bastard. You're no friend of my father's. What the hell are you doing here?"

SHERIFF MITCH TANNER sat in his patrol car outside the *Timber Falls Courier* trying to decide what to do about Charity. A few weeks ago he'd almost lost her to a killer. Bud Farnsworth was dead, but Mitch feared that the man who killed him was even more dangerous.

Whatever Charity wrote in her newspaper would set Wade Dennison off. The owner of Dennison Ducks was a powerful man in this town and he used that power and money to get his way. Men like that often thought they were above the law.

One thing was for certain, Bud would never have come up with the idea of kidnapping the Dennison baby by himself. Mitch suspected he'd been paid.

That's why Mitch had subpoenaed Wade Dennison's and Bud Farnsworth's financial records. Wade's attorney had held up the process for two weeks, arguing the case was closed. The kidnapper was dead.

But Mitch wasn't giving up because he knew in his heart that the true kidnapper, the person who'd planned the whole thing and paid Bud Farnsworth to snatch Angela Dennison, was still out there. Still walking around thinking he'd gotten away with it.

A tap on the glass made Mitch jump. "Jesse," he said rolling down his window. "I wish you'd quit sneaking around in the dark."

Jesse's smile was all Tanner dimples. He was just a little shorter than Mitch, stockier though, with long black hair pulled back in a ponytail, a gold earring in his right ear and handsome to a fault. "Hey, little bro. Spying on your woman?"

Mitch shook his head, not wanting to talk about Charity, especially with his brother. It was no secret that Jesse wished Charity had fallen for him. Mitch was just getting used to having his brother back in town. There'd been a time when he believed his wild, older brother was headed straight for a life of crime.

But Jesse had come back to Timber Falls a few weeks ago and really seemed to be trying to make up for his past mistakes. Mitch couldn't help but respect his brother for that. Jesse had also brought Mitch and their father closer.

"I thought you'd like to know," Jesse said now. "I just saw Wade Dennison move lock, stock and barrel into one of the units out at Florie's."

Mitch stared at him. "Nina's old unit? Aries?"

Florie, a self-proclaimed psychic, had turned her motel into bungalow rentals years ago and named each of the twelve for the signs of the Zodiac. "What's up with that?" Mitch asked.

"Looks like Daisy threw him out."

What were the chances of that? Nil. Unless Daisy had something on Wade that she was holding over his head. Like she knew he was behind the kidnapping of their daughter, Angela. Or Daisy and her lover's daughter.

Mitch looked at Jesse, both of them no doubt thinking the same thing. If Angela had been a love child, then the father of that baby might very well be their own father, Lee Tanner. Lee and Daisy had had an affair in the year before Angela was born.

"How'd Wade seem?" Mitch asked, even more worried about Charity now.

Jesse shook his head. "He didn't look good. I'd say the man was about at the end of his rope. Can you imagine what will happen when this gets around town?"

And it wouldn't take long for that to happen given that Charity's Aunt Florie was one of the biggest gossips in town. And then there was Charity.

Mitch groaned at the thought of Charity's newspaper hitting the streets in the morning. There would be fireworks, sure as hell. He just hoped no one got killed.

"Damn," he swore, wondering if he should pay Wade a visit tonight. By the next day, Mitch was pretty sure he'd have the financial reports on Wade Dennison and Bud Farnsworth. And he figured he'd be paying Wade a visit once he had proof in hand anyway. No reason to court trouble tonight.

The patrol car radio squawked. Mitch took the call. A man had been found unconscious at the bottom of a cliff, not far from the recent Bigfoot sighting spot, and dropped off at the hospital. No ID.

Mitch turned to his brother. "Sounds like one of those damned Bigfoot hunters fell off a cliff and is over at the hospital."

"You need any help? I was headed home but I could tag along."

Mitch shook his head. In remote areas of Oregon, sheriffs worked alone—unless they needed to call in state investigators for help—or they could deputize someone locally for the short term.

"Later, then," Jesse said and headed toward his motorcycle parked in the alley.

Chapter Four

"Rozalyn! Have you lost your mind?" Emily cried.

Roz stood glaring at Ford Lancaster, so angry she couldn't speak.

This man sitting in the house that had once been her home was *Ford Lancaster,* the man who had ruined her father's reputation. The man who had almost killed her at the waterfall. The man who had lied about being Liam's friend. The man who had finagled his way into the guest house.

And if that wasn't bad enough, he'd...*kissed* her!

"Do you have any idea who this man is you're letting stay in the guest house?" she demanded, turning her hard-eyed gaze on Emily.

"Of course I do. Ford Lancaster. He's a scientist up here doing some research and a friend of *your* father's."

Emily never ceased to amaze her. "This man is no friend of his. Quite the opposite."

"Wait a minute," Ford interrupted loudly. "Who the hell is your father?"

"Liam Sawyer," Rozalyn snapped. "But if you really were his friend, wouldn't you know that?"

"You'd think so, wouldn't you?" Ford stared at her. And just when he thought his luck couldn't get any worse. Liam Sawyer's daughter. *I'll be damned.*

His gaze went to her lips. Her mouth was a wide, full mouth, sensual. He wished he'd taken more time with that kiss in the garden. All that kiss had done was whet his appetite. But if he got another chance—

Then his gaze drifted up to her eyes. He couldn't help but chuckle. If looks could kill, he'd be pushing up daisies right now. He didn't even want to think about his chances of ever getting to kiss this woman again.

"You think this is funny?" she demanded.

"Not really." Ironic? Tragic? Just his luck that this crazy doe-eyed strawberry blonde was Liam Sawyer's daughter.

He couldn't help but think about earlier when he'd had her in his arms. Unconsciously, he rubbed his shin and saw the hint of a smile curve her lips. No question about it, she was a menace and now she was his.

Why hadn't someone told him Liam had a daughter? Didn't he remember Rozalyn saying something about it having been years since she'd been up here? Yeah. So maybe that was the reason he was taken completely unaware.

He knew the old man had remarried and had a couple of adult stepchildren—but a *daughter* who looked like this? Worse, a daughter who was obviously going to make things harder for him? Oh, hell. This changed things considerably.

"I can't believe you'd be so rude to our guest," Emily said, sounding close to tears.

"This man is not *our* guest," Rozalyn said, narrowing those eyes at him with obvious venom.

He figured her bite was probably worse than her bark—or her kick. Clearly, Rozalyn was a woman to be reckoned with.

"Why don't you tell us, *Mr. Lancaster,* what you're *really* doing here?" She glared at him as if she hadn't missed him giving her the once-over. Those big brown eyes were hot with anger and a clear warning.

This wasn't going to be easy. But there were ways. Even with a woman like her. A woman who thought she didn't need a man.

"I guess the cat has his tongue. Mr. Lancaster here is the man who wrote the article about my father, calling him a liar and a fraud," Rozalyn said, still glaring at him.

"What article?" Emily asked.

"The article that accused him of faking photographs of Bigfoot and perpetuating a hoax," Rozalyn said. "It was my father's word against Ford Lancaster and his so-called experts."

Not exactly, Ford thought. There'd been another man with Liam Sawyer, another witness, who had also been discredited. And that article had been years ago. "I need to talk to you," he said to Rozalyn as he got to his feet.

She shot him a when-hell-freezes-over look.

"Maybe it was another Ford Lancaster," Emily suggested.

"How many Ford Lancasters do you think there are?" Rozalyn demanded.

A maid appeared in the doorway behind Rozalyn. "Excuse me. There's someone here to see you."

No one seemed to hear her.

"Wasn't that article years ago?" Drew asked.

"Yes," Emily chimed in. "Who would even remember, let alone care—"

"I remember and I care," Rozalyn shot back. "So does my father. Do you know the man you married at all? Or what matters to him? Do you have any idea what that article did to him?"

"I'm sure Mother didn't know Mr. Lancaster wrote the article when she offered him the guest house," Drew said.

"Of course not," Emily said. "I would never do anything to hurt Liam. Or you, Rozalyn, dear. He told me he was a friend of Liam's, and since there was no place in town to stay..."

"Excuse me. There is someone here to see you," the maid repeated.

"Ilsa, can't you see we're about to have dinner?" Emily snapped. "Tell whoever it is to come back some other time and close the doors behind you." She shot Rozalyn a look as if to say now everyone in town will be talking about your behavior.

"It's the sheriff. He wants to speak to Rozalyn," Ilse persisted.

"Rozalyn? Why would the sheriff want to talk to her?" Emily said as if it was the prince at the door with a glass slipper. "Oh Rozalyn, you didn't already involve the sheriff in our affairs, did you?"

"What do you want me to tell the sheriff?" the maid asked nervously. "Should I tell him to come back?"

"No, Rozalyn and I will both see him," Ford said. The maid turned tail and disappeared down the hall. "If you will excuse me," he said to Emily and the others. "I apologize, Emily, but Rozalyn and I really do need to talk to the sheriff."

Ford took Roz's arm and practically dragged her out into the hallway, closing the French doors firmly behind them.

"We have to talk," he whispered. "I had no idea Liam had a daughter. But now that I do... I'm here because I think your father is in trouble." He held up a hand to ward off her questions. "I will explain later. Right now we need to see the sheriff. I assume you called him about earlier and that's why he's here?"

She jerked free, but he could see her anger deflating at his words. "My father's in trouble?"

"Possibly. Look, you called the sheriff about what you thought you saw at the falls, right? Let's get this over with, then you can tell me what you think of me at length," he said reasonably. "And I'll tell me everything I know about your father."

She obviously didn't feel like being reasonable. "I want to know why my father is in trouble and what that has to do with you and I want to know now," she said, keeping her voice down.

He groaned. "There isn't time now." He looked past her to where the sheriff was standing and watching them, then lowered his head and said quietly, "If you say anything to the sheriff, I'll deny it and you will never know why I'm here.''

Her eyes flared with anger.

"Let's tell the sheriff what you saw," he added, loud enough that the officer of the law could hear.

Her body trembled with obvious rage as he took her arm and drew her toward the front door and the sheriff.

"Mitch," she said when she saw the uniformed man at the door. She broke free of Ford's grasp and rushed toward the sheriff.

Mitch? She knew him? Of course she might. She must have lived here until her mother had died. Sure. The conversation he'd overheard in the garden was starting to make sense. So was her relationship with the people in the dining room.

Ford met the sheriff's interested gaze, and felt his insides tighten. The sheriff had come for more than just a statement from Rozalyn about a possible suicide at Lost Creek Falls. Ford stood back, watching the sheriff's face and Rozalyn's body language. She hugged the cop and they exchanged a few pleasantries, then Ford heard the words he'd been dreading.

"A fall? Is Dad all right?"

The sheriff had taken off his hat. "He's in a coma, Roz."

"We have to get him flown out to Eugene, to the hospital there—"

The sheriff was shaking his head. "His condition is such that the doc says he can't be moved right now."

"I'm going to the hospital to see him," she said,

pushing past Ford as he joined them. She ran up the stairs, no doubt to get her purse and car keys.

Ford found himself under the sheriff's intense scrutiny.

"I don't believe we've met," the lawman said.

"No, I'm Ford Lancaster." From the sheriff's negative reaction it was obvious Ford's reputation had preceded him.

The sheriff started to ask him something, but behind them, the dining room doors burst open. Ford was surprised it had taken Emily this long.

"What's going on?" she demanded.

As the sheriff filled her in, she burst into tears and called for Drew. Suzanne finally came out seeming more irritated than anything else. "Liam's been hurt," Emily cried. "Drew, will you drive me to the hospital?"

"Of course, Mother," he said.

"I just need to change," she said looking down at her shoes. Ford would guess she didn't want to get them wet.

"I'll stay here, Mother," Suzanne said. "In case anyone calls."

Why would anyone call? Ford wondered. Suzanne still held her wineglass. She drained it and turned back to the dining room. A look passed between Suzanne and Emily before a tearful Emily ascended the stairs with Drew following after her.

Ford noticed that Emily hadn't asked about Liam's accident. "Where was he found?" he asked as the others left him and the sheriff alone.

"Up Maple Creek. When did you get to town?"

"Rozalyn followed me in from Oakridge."

"Then you saw the jumper at Lost Creek Falls?" The sheriff sounded surprised.

Ford shook his head. "I'm not sure there was a jumper. I think she might have…imagined it. She's been pretty upset about her father—and with good reason it seems. Who found him?"

"Some Bigfoot hunters. They dropped him at the hospital." The sheriff glanced up the stairs as Rozalyn hurried down.

Ford reached for the keys dangling from her fingers. "I'm driving you."

"I'd like to have a few words with you at the hospital," the sheriff was saying to Ford.

"No problem." He took the keys from Rozalyn before she could protest. The sheriff raised a brow, probably expecting Rozalyn to put up a fight. "We'll see you at the hospital, Sheriff," Ford said.

Roz let Ford open the passenger side door of her SUV for her, then watched him hurry around to slide behind the wheel.

She leaned back against the seat, fighting panic, as she gave him the four-block directions to the Timber Falls hospital. Her father was in a coma. Mitch said he'd fallen from a cliff up Maple Creek Road and had been found by some Bigfoot hunters. Hadn't she known something had happened to him? If only she'd come sooner. If only—

Her gaze swung to Ford, suddenly remembering what he had said. "What did you mean when you told me my father was in trouble?" she asked as they neared the hospital.

He shot her a look, then turned back to his driving. "Let's just go to the hospital and find out what we can for now, all right?"

"No," she said, sitting up a little straighter. "You said it was the reason you were here. Did you mean Timber Falls? Or the house?"

"There isn't time to get into this right now. I'll tell you everything," he said, meeting her gaze. "After you see your father."

Ford swung the SUV into the hospital emergency entrance. Roz closed her eyes tightly for a moment, trying to hold it together. She had to be strong—for her father. She'd deal with Ford later.

Before he had the car parked, she was out and running toward the emergency room door. He caught up with her in time to open the door for her.

She rushed into the small hospital entry with him right behind her. The nurse's station was empty.

Her heart dropped. What if her father had gotten worse? What if—

She could make out a steady beep coming from down the dim hallway. She rushed toward the sound, the hurried footfalls of her and Ford echoing on the linoleum floor, as she prayed her father was alive even if still in a coma.

At the open doorway, Roz had a passing impression of a nurse and a doctor, both dressed in white beside a hospital bed. The nurse was round and rosy-cheeked with a halo of white hair. The doctor was blond, late forties, nice-looking.

Roz looked past both to the bandaged man lying in

the bed, monitors making soft bleating noises, a respirator breathing in and out, in and out.

Her throat constricted at the sight of her father. He looked as white as the sheets and so incredibly frail but he was still alive! Thank God.

"How is he?" Roz asked, rushing into the room.

"No change, but he's holding his own," the nurse said. She smiled when she saw Roz as if she knew her. "I'm so glad you're here and I know your father is, too." Her eyes twinkled. "He knows you've come to see him, don't worry about that."

"Thank you," Roz said. "I'm—"

"Rozalyn," she said and smiled more broadly. "You look just like your mother. I'm Kate Clark. I know you don't remember me, but I was at your birth. Don't worry about your father. He's in good hands. I'll be here all night."

"I won't, knowing you're taking care of him," Roz said.

"This is Dr. Harris," the nurse said.

The doctor had been looking at her father's chart. He looked up and frowned. "Who are you?" He sounded irritated.

"I'm his daughter, Rozalyn," she said looking down at her dad. She fought back tears as she whispered, "I'm here, Dad," and squeezed his hand. No response. She glanced up, expecting to see Ford in the doorway. But he was gone. "He's in a coma?"

The doctor nodded. "That's typical with this kind of head injury."

"The sheriff said he fell?" Roz asked.

"Probably slipped. Didn't fall far, I would guess, but struck his head on something," the doctor said.

"Who brought him in?" Roz looked at the nurse, who shook her head, then the doctor.

"They didn't leave names," he said. "Just out-of-towners up here looking for Bigfoot. Your father really needs his rest—" Dr. Harris broke off when he saw Ford reappear in the doorway again. The doctor put down the clipboard and started to leave the room. "Please keep your visit short."

He had reached the doorway when Emily and Drew rushed past Ford and into the room.

"Oh, no!" Emily cried, stopping in the center of the room to cover her face. "How bad is it, Dr. Harris?"

"I'm optimistic and you should be, too, Mrs. Sawyer. He's a strong, stubborn man. He won't give up easily," the doctor said. "I was going to call you with the news but the sheriff insisted on doing it."

"Yes," Emily said and glanced at Roz. "I guess he wanted to tell Liam's daughter first."

Rozalyn hardly noticed the bitterness in the woman's tone. She was too surprised that Emily seemed to know the doctor. But the new Mrs. Sawyer had been in town for over a month. Emily probably knew everyone in Timber Falls by now.

"Oh, Drew," Emily said as he moved to put his arm around her shoulders.

Roz looked up at Ford who was still in the doorway. He motioned for her. "I'll give you a moment alone with Liam," she said as she squeezed her dad's hand, then laid it gently back on the bed beside him and left the room, surprised to find both Mitch and Ford waiting for her out in the hall. She could feel the tension between them, and could only guess what had been going on.

Ford closed the hospital room door but watched through the window as Mitch said, "Lancaster here feels your father needs protection."

Her gaze leaped to Ford. He didn't seem to notice. He was watching the group in the hospital room, looking worried, his jaw tight. He'd said her father was in trouble *before* Mitch told her Liam was in the hospital. It was almost as if Ford had been expecting this to happen. Why was that? She remembered his promise to tell her everything as soon as they left here.

She stared at Ford, reminding herself of all the reasons she shouldn't trust the man. And yet something in his worried expression—

"I think that's a good idea, Mitch," she said, making the decision not only to keep quiet about what Ford had told her—but to trust that he had his reasons for wanting her father protected.

Mitch was staring at her in obvious surprise. "Why?"

"Is there someone I can hire to stay with him, not let him out of sight even for a moment?" Ford asked, finally looking at the sheriff. "Is there someone in town who would be reliable and willing to take the job? Someone you trust?"

But Mitch was still looking at Roz. "You think your father is in danger?" he asked.

She nodded. "I can't explain it, but I do, Mitch."

He let out a long sigh and looked at Ford. "I know someone. My brother, Jesse Tanner. No one will get past Jesse to Liam. But I need to know why you feel Liam needs that kind of protection."

"Let's just say I have a bad feeling that his fall wasn't an accident," Ford said.

Roz must have looked as shocked as Mitch.

"You have any proof of that?" the sheriff asked.

"Not yet," Ford said. "But if you want to keep him alive, then I suggest you call your brother and get him up here. If you're sure he can be trusted."

"I'd trust him with my life and Liam's," Mitch said.

Ford looked to Roz, then nodded. "Call him." He glanced back through the hospital room window as if he wasn't moving an inch until Jesse Tanner arrived to take over.

"Can I have a word with you?" Mitch asked Roz as he stepped down the hall, pulled out his cell and punched in a series of numbers. When the line answered, he said, "It's me," and briefly explained the situation. A few seconds later, he disconnected. "Jesse's on his way. I've deputized him so there won't be any question as to his authority for being here."

"Thanks, Mitch."

"Look, Roz, I don't know what the deal is with you and Lancaster—"

"There's nothing between us. I just don't want to take any chances with my dad, that's all," she said.

He nodded, but she could tell he wasn't buying it for a minute.

"It just isn't like him to fall off a cliff," she said and shuddered at the thought of how long he'd lain there before he'd been found. She couldn't bear the thought that he'd been in pain, worse that he may have been pushed, may have even seen his assailant.

"No, it's not like Liam, but accidents do happen," Mitch said. "What's odd is that I was up Maple Creek Road earlier tonight and I didn't see his pickup and camper. Is it possible someone dropped him off at the trailhead?"

That *was* odd. "I don't know. His truck isn't at the house. Emily said he took it when he left two weeks ago."

"I'm sure it will turn up," Mitch assured her. "And don't worry. Your dad's going to pull through. You know how tough he is. Then he'll tell us just what happened."

She nodded and smiled through her tears. She was counting on it, she thought as she looked down the hall at Ford standing outside her father's hospital room. In the meantime, any answers were going to have to come from Ford Lancaster.

She balked at the idea but still couldn't wait until Jesse Tanner arrived so she could find out why the man who'd tried to destroy Liam in print years ago was now trying to save him.

"How long have you been sheriff?" she asked Mitch, not wanting to go back down to her father's room until Emily and Drew were finished.

"Pretty much since Sheriff Hudson retired."

She knew the sheriff had retired shortly after her mother's death. She tried not to think about that right now and looked into Mitch's handsome face instead, then at his ring finger.

He laughed. "No, Charity hasn't lassoed me yet—but not for lack of trying."

When she and Charity used to play house, Charity was always married to Mitch Tanner while Roz's pretend husband was not only nameless but also faceless.

"Have you seen Charity?" he asked.

She shook her head. "Not for a while."

"I know she'd love to see you. She has breakfast every morning at Betty's."

Roz nodded. "I'd love to see her, too."

Mitch pulled out a small notebook and pen. "Why don't we go over what you saw at Lost Creek Falls while we're waiting."

Roz hugged herself against the memory as she told him.

"What made you think it was a woman?" he asked, taking notes.

She shook her head. "All I really saw was the bright yellow raincoat but at one point I thought I saw long blond hair. It was too dark to make out much." She hesitated. "And it happened so fast."

"Lancaster says he didn't see anything."

She shook her head ruefully. "He thought I was going to jump and tried to save me. He almost killed me instead."

Mitch didn't look pleased to hear this. "Where is he staying?"

"Our guest house. Emily invited him. Says she didn't know who he was, thought he was a friend of Liam's." Obviously Ford had led her to believe that.

Mitch raised a brow. "What is Lancaster doing in town?"

She shook her head, watching Ford. She wished she knew.

The sheriff put his notebook away. "I'll drive up to the falls and take a look tonight but doubt there is anything I can do until morning." They both knew that at this point he would just be retrieving the body. She shuddered at the thought. If there really was a body to retrieve. And shuddered again.

"Lancaster say how long he's staying?" Mitch asked following her gaze down the hall to Ford.

"No." He hadn't told her anything. Yet.

Mitch pulled off his hat and raked a hand through his dark hair. "Come on, Roz, you drove all the way up here from Seattle because you were worried about your father. Why?"

She told him about the message her dad had left on her answering machine. "He sounded upset. I tried to call him back but couldn't reach him. No one had heard from him at the house. Of course I was worried."

Mitch put his hat back on. "Emily have any idea why Liam might have been upset?"

"I didn't tell her about the call." She could feel the sheriff's gaze on her. "But I asked her if they'd had an argument. She denied it. I think she's lying. I think something happened between the two of them before he left."

Mitch was looking down the hall again. Emily came out of Liam's room with Drew at her side. Dr. Harris came out of another room and led Emily and

Drew down the hallway in the opposite direction. They disappeared into one of the offices.

"Be careful, okay?" Mitch said quietly, watching after them.

Roz looked over at him in surprise. "You think I'm right?"

"I don't know what to think," Mitch said. "But I'd watch Lancaster." He smiled over at her. "You're too smart to fall for any line he might try to give you, right?"

Right. She turned as the front door of the hospital opened and a dark broad-shouldered man with a ponytail and a black biker jacket came through the door. It had been years since she'd seen Jesse Tanner. Mitch's older brother had been in reform school most of the time. This was the man Mitch had guarding her father?

"Hey, Rozie," Jesse said coming toward her. He had the Tanner black hair and eyes and those deep dimples. Only Jesse was handsome in a dangerous way. He also appeared very capable of keeping her father safe.

"Sorry about your papa. But don't worry. I'll see that no one does him any harm as long as I'm around."

She trusted Mitch's judgment. "I believe you," she said. "Thank you, Jesse."

"My pleasure." He gave her a grin. There was a rakishness about Jesse, a raw sexuality. This man was a danger to women. Just like another man she'd recently met, she thought, looking down the hall to where Ford lounged against the wall, eyes hooded, his body looking deceptively relaxed.

She had the feeling that he could spring like a big cat at a moment's notice. He was watching her father's room. But she knew he was also aware of her. Just as she was him.

"I WANT SOME ANSWERS," Rozalyn demanded the moment they walked out of the hospital.

Ford was surprised she'd been able to hold her tongue that long. He opened the passenger side door of her SUV for her. She got in without seeming to notice he intended to drive. Without a word, he slid behind the wheel, started the car and headed down the street.

"You really think someone purposely tried to kill my father?"

"I just feel better with a guard in his room, all right? Just until we find out what happened," Ford said. "Like I said—"

"You have a bad feeling. I heard. Why didn't you tell the sheriff what you told me?"

He pulled up in front of Betty's Café. It was early enough the place was still open but late enough there were only a few people inside still eating.

"What are you doing?" she asked as he shut off the engine and started to get out.

"Getting something to eat. I'm still hungry. You might remember I didn't get any dinner." As he got out, he heard her open her door and follow him.

"How can you even think about food at a time like

this?'' she demanded, catching up with him before he opened the café door for her.

''I'm sorry about your dad but we both need to eat if we're going to keep up our strength so we can find out what happened to him.'' He held open the door. ''After you.''

She mumbled something under her breath but entered, going to a booth at the back out of earshot from the other diners. He followed her, glad to see her angry. Earlier when she'd been with her father, she'd looked broken. He needed her to be strong and if being angry was what it took, he could oblige.

He also needed her to trust him. That, he realized as he slid in the booth across from her, was going to take some doing.

A YOUNG WAITRESS Roz didn't recognize brought them menus. Roz didn't even bother to open hers, knowing she wouldn't be able to eat a bite. She was worried about her father, although knowing that Jesse Tanner was in the hospital room watching over him helped. Now if her father would just come out of his coma—

''Give us two western omelettes, extra cheese, and two cups of black coffee,'' Ford said without opening his menu, either. He didn't even bother to ask Roz if she would have liked cream.

''Well?'' she demanded the moment the waitress was out of earshot. ''You got me here, now talk.''

''Are you always this impatient?'' he asked.

''No, I'm actually on my best behavior. You wouldn't want to see me when I'm not,'' she snapped.

He smiled, obviously recognizing his own words from earlier.

He wasn't bad-looking when he smiled. Under the bright fluorescent lights of Betty's Café, she could see featherings of gray at his temples and tiny laugh lines around his sea-green eyes. He had a rugged look about him as if he'd spent a lot of time outdoors.

It surprised her. He was nothing like she had pictured him in her mind all these years. He must have been very young when he'd written the article about her father, she realized.

The waitress returned with the coffees.

Roz cradled the mug of hot coffee in her hands, needing the warmth as she sat waiting, glaring across the table at a man she had hated since the age of sixteen without ever knowing anything more about him than his name. Ford Lancaster. Her idea of the devil incarnate.

She was sixteen when the article had come out about her father. She felt cold inside as she remembered how it had devastated him.

Liam Sawyer had been on a camping trip with a friend when the two had stumbled across a large creature in the woods. Her father, who always had his camera, had hit the motordrive. But his hands had been shaking from shock and surprise, and the photographs of the creature were out of focus, the image blurred.

But still the photographs had been big news when they'd hit print. Liam had believed that his discovery would change the world's attitude about Bigfoot's existence.

That seemed the case, until Ford Lancaster called in some so-called experts to denounce the photographs as an elaborate hoax instigated by her father.

No one had believed Liam or his friend after Ford Lancaster's article came out and the news hit the papers. No one except people who knew him. But Liam Sawyer had never gotten over the humiliation. Whenever there was a Bigfoot sighting in the years since, his photographs and the incident were always mentioned.

Her father had sworn that he'd get irrefutable proof of Bigfoot's existence or die trying. But as many times as he had returned to the Cascades, he'd never seen the creature again.

Some years later another photographer had admitted that his Bigfoot photos had been faked, casting even more suspicion on her father's photos.

Roz had spent over a decade hating Ford Lancaster and now he was sitting across the table from her.

Ford didn't seem to notice her glaring in his direction. He was without a doubt the most arrogant, rude, obnoxious man—

"I'm sorry about the way I acted earlier," he said, lifting that pale gaze to meet hers. "At the waterfall."

She shrugged and looked down at her coffee, a little thrown by the fact that he'd apologized. Not so thrown that she didn't have a comeback. "Now that I know who you are, I wouldn't expect anything less than your behavior at the waterfall."

He pretended to be wounded. "Seriously, I'm trying to change."

"Not having much luck, huh?"

He smiled. He had a nice mouth, but then she already knew that from earlier in the garden.

"Stop stalling. Don't make me sorry I covered for you with the sheriff."

He shook his head, still smiling as if he found her amusing. "Why did you?"

"Why did you lie to Emily about being a friend of my father's?"

"What makes you so sure it's a lie?"

She reached into her purse and pulled out her cell phone and started to dial the sheriff. He reached across the table and gently touched her hand holding the phone. She met his gaze.

"Can you sit still long enough for me to tell you my way?" He shook his head, answering for her. "Then I'll try to make it quick. I was twenty-four when I wrote the article about your father's photographs." She did the math. That made him thirty-six now, eight years older than she was. "It wasn't just about your father. There was someone else with him when he took those photos."

"John Wells." Her father's friend.

Ford nodded. "His name is John *Ford* Wells. He's my father."

Her jaw dropped. "How could that be since his name is Wells and yours—"

"My parents divorced when I was four. My mother remarried. I hardly ever saw my biological father—just enough to…resent the hell out of him."

She felt her eyes widen with understanding.

He nodded. "It wasn't your father I was going after in that article. It was mine."

She was dumbstruck. "You did that to your own father."

"Yeah, well, I'm a jerk, but you already know that about me." He met her gaze, his eyes the color of a warm Caribbean lagoon she'd once photographed for one of her books.

"That makes it easy for you, doesn't it."

"No, actually, nothing has been easy." He seemed to turn serious and she felt her breath catch at his next words. "John Wells hadn't been well. I was with him the day Liam called." He nodded. "I took the call. Liam sounded…scared. He wasn't making a lot of sense, almost as if he'd been drinking."

She was shaking her head. "My father never has more than a glass of wine with dinner."

"You want to hear this or not?"

She made a face at him and he continued, "He sounded as if he'd been drinking. He said he couldn't get through to the sheriff, that he was in trouble, that he'd found something. I thought he said bones."

"Bones?"

Ford nodded. "Then he said what I thought was, 'John, they're trying to kill me' and we were cut off."

She felt a shiver but couldn't help being skeptical given who was telling the story. "Why would my father call *you?*"

"I answered the phone. I guess I sounded enough like John Wells, and that Liam just assumed—"

"Why didn't you give the phone to your father?"

Ford chewed at his cheek for a moment, glancing out the window before settling that blue-green gaze on her again. "Because John Ford Wells had died just minutes before Liam's call."

Chapter Five

Ford watched her eyes fill with tears. "I'm so sorry about your father," she said and reached across the table to cover his hand.

"It's all right," he said taking back his hand. He didn't want her sympathy. It made him feel guilty and he felt guilty enough already. "We were never close."

"That's too bad." She looked down, her brown eyes swimming in tears, as she cupped her coffee mug.

He could see that she was thinking about her father, worrying that she might lose him. They were obviously very close. Or had been before his recent marriage, Ford guessed.

Her gaze lifted to his. "Why didn't you call the sheriff right away?"

"I thought your father was drunk. But the more I thought about it... So I came up here determined to get to the bottom of it."

She was eyeing him suspiciously, obviously realizing there was a lot more to it.

"Look, I called your father's house. I talked to Emily. She told me everything was fine, that she expected to hear from Liam at any time and not to concern myself.''

"Emily," Rozalyn said under her breath like a curse.

"My old man said Liam Sawyer was one of the toughest men he ever knew and one of the best.''

Hope shimmered along with her tears now. "He is something for his age, isn't he?''

Ford nodded.

She shook her head as if she found it all too unbelievable. "Why would anyone hurt him?''

"If he really did find bones—''

"What kind of bones would be worth trying to kill a man over?''

Ford hesitated, then lowered his voice. "Given what Liam had been doing up in the mountains, I'd say Bigfoot bones.''

Roz stared at him as if too shocked to speak. "Excuse me? You scientists have discredited the thousands of Bigfoot-like creature sightings around the world saying that if such a beast existed, then why hadn't a skeleton ever been found. Are you telling me now that *you* think it's possible he could have found a Bigfoot skeleton?''

"Possible. Not probable.'' Hadn't he been waiting most of his life for this? He didn't believe and yet, God knew, he wanted to.

Roz eyed him, trying to put her finger on her misgivings about Ford Lancaster. Misgivings, hell. She didn't trust him. He was the enemy. Wasn't he?

"Why would anyone try to kill my father over Bigfoot bones?'' she asked, still wondering why he hadn't gone to the sheriff.

"You aren't really that naive, are you? A Bigfoot skeleton would be an incredible find. It would set the scientific world on its ear.'' Excitement crept into his voice and his sea-green eyes shone in the café lights. "The bones could prove to be hominid, a subspecies of us, human.''

"You make it sound as if you believe they exist,'' she said, surprised by the enthusiasm she heard in his voice.

"It's possible,'' he said slowly. "After all the Ishii, the last of a Stone Age Indian tribe, had remained hidden in a canyon only eight miles from Oroville, California, in the early 1900s until they voluntarily came out and made themselves known. The mountain gorilla wasn't proven to exist until 1902. It would make the person who found the bones famous. Not to mention rich.''

"Rich?''

"Those bones are worth a fortune,'' he said. "Not just in the rewards being offered for definitive proof that such a creature exists, but to private collectors.''

She'd never thought of a find like that in monetary terms because she knew her father wouldn't have, either. "My father would never have sold them. He would have donated them to a museum.''

"But that doesn't mean that someone else out there doesn't realize their value and intends to cash in on the find.''

"You're saying that someone found out about the bones and—'' A sob choked off her words.

"Liam sounded like he was running scared when he called."

Running scared. That's how she felt right now. "And you think he's still in danger?" she said, brushing at her tears.

"If the bones are Bigfoot bones, then your father is in danger as long as someone thinks he is going to tell about the discovery."

He reached over and touched her hand, sending a jolt through her. He jerked his hand back, looking embarrassed as he picked up his cup, his gaze set on the coffee.

She stared at him, her heart beating too fast, and all he'd done was touch her. Who was this man who could be so kind one moment and so awful the next? And why did her body have to react this way with Ford Lancaster of all people?

He must feel the same way, she thought as she watched him stare into his coffee. Touching her had been a mistake. No kidding.

She took a drink of her own coffee and realized her hands were shaking.

He didn't look up as he said, "Until the bones are found—"

"But by now, wouldn't the person have gotten the bones out of the woods?"

"I don't think so or we would have heard about it. The bones could be too large to move. Or embedded in the rock. I don't know. Maybe your father found something portable like a skeleton and hid it. But if someone had the bones in their possession, they would have made the announcement by now."

"You think my father might have hidden what he found?" Roz realized her dad had been making some really bad decisions lately. Marrying Emily. Bringing her to the house here at Timber Falls. Maybe he had hidden the bones, knowing someone was following him. She just hoped it wouldn't cost him his life.

"Until Liam regains consciousness we have no way of knowing," Ford was saying. "Or until I find the bones. The sheriff told me where Liam was found. At least I have a place to start looking in the morning."

"I'm going with you."

His gaze locked with hers. "It's too dangerous. If I'm right and your father's fall wasn't an accident, then whoever did it won't hesitate to do the same thing to you if given a chance."

"You don't know this area like I do," she argued. "My dad has taken me up in those mountains since I was old enough to ride in a backpack. I probably know more about Bigfoot hunting than you do and I know my father. You need me."

She wanted to find those bones before whoever had hurt her father profited from them. She also wanted to find the person who'd done this to her father. If his fall really hadn't been an accident. If Ford Lancaster was telling her the truth. "I am going with you," she told him. "So don't even try to stop me."

She caught something in his gaze just an instant before he said, "I should have known I couldn't talk you out of it." What was it that she'd seen in his eyes? Relief? Or triumph?

She took a sip of her coffee, watching him over

the rim of her cup as he ate. "What I don't understand is why you would risk your life to help my father."

He smiled as if he'd been expecting the question. "Let's just say I owe him for the article I wrote on him."

"You could just write a retraction," she said. "Instead of risking your life."

He shook his head. "The photographs your father took were too blurry to prove anything one way or the other. The experts I had look at them were as convinced as I was that they'd been faked." He held up a hand quickly to keep her from biting his head off. "Look, I didn't know your father. Or mine, for that matter. And yes, I did have an ax to grind. I'm not proud of it. But like I said, that's the past. There's no going back and changing that."

That seemed a bit too simple, but she let it ride. After all Ford's father had been Liam's best friend— and had been hurt by the article as well. Maybe Ford also wanted to make up some things to his own father.

"I think we should keep this just between the two of us," Ford said, looking up at her. "It sounds like there are enough people out there searching for Bigfoot as it is without word of this getting out. If we stand any hope of finding the bones—"

"And the person who injured my father," she said.

"Yes. If we announce what we're looking for, we'll scare him off. Or force him to move quicker to get the bones out before we can find them."

Their food arrived. To her surprise, Roz realized she was hungry after all. She'd felt so helpless at the hospital but now there seemed to be something she could do besides pray and wait beside her father's hospital bed for him to recover.

They ate in silence, wolfing down their meals as if neither had eaten in weeks. By the time they finished, it was getting late.

"I want to stop by the hospital and see my father again."

"I thought you might. Mind if I go with you?"

She didn't mind in the least. In fact, she was glad for the company. Ever since he'd told her about the danger he thought her father was in, she'd found herself looking over her shoulder. She wanted to make sure Liam was safe—and hoped he'd be conscious by the time they got there.

Jesse Tanner was sprawled in a chair in the hospital room when she walked in. He nodded at her as she entered the room. Ford stayed in the doorway.

Roz pulled up a chair beside her father's bed. "I'm here, Dad," she whispered and squeezed his hand. No response. She began to talk softly to him, talking about the past, reliving memories she'd buried ten years ago when her mother died. He never moved, never gave any indication he heard her.

She was crying softly by the time she finally stood and let go of his hand. "I'll be back." She needed to find out what had happened to him. Ford was right about that, she thought, glancing toward the door.

But even as she thought it, she wondered again at Ford's motivations. What was it about the man that made her so suspicious of him? Was it just the article he'd written so many years ago or something else? Something she couldn't quite put her finger on.

Roz hadn't realized how tired she was until she and Ford walked out of the hospital. The night was dark, the clouds damp and low. In the distance lightning flashed above the tree line.

"I'm going to walk back," Ford said and handed her the keys as thunder rumbled softly to the west. "Will you be all right?"

"It's only a few blocks," Roz said, surprised she was a little disappointed he wasn't coming with her.

"I'll see you in the morning. Good night."

When she drove away, he was still standing in front of the hospital. She wondered if he was worried about security for her father or if he just wanted some time alone. She could understand that.

Roz thought of her father and felt a chill. Who was it he had to fear? It could be anyone...

Even Ford Lancaster?

As a car came around the dark corner at the end of the street from the hospital, Ford stepped back into the shadows. A sports car pulled up next to the emergency room entrance. Drew Lane got out and looked around before walking to the passenger side and opening the car door. His mother emerged, also glancing around before rushing inside.

Drew held the car door open as Suzanne Lane stumbled out from the small space in the back. She shoved away his offered hand for help, obviously intoxicated, and wound her way toward the hospital entrance. "I don't know why I had to be here," she said to her mother.

Emily said something under her breath that Ford couldn't make out but whatever it was, it wasn't nice.

Drew followed the two women inside. Neither noticed Ford in the shadows watching them. Or heard him enter the hospital a few minutes later behind them.

"Who are you?" he heard Emily exclaim from Liam's room.

Ford smiled to himself as he quietly stepped into the room after the trio. Jesse was still sprawled in the chair in the corner of Liam Sawyer's room but Ford didn't doubt from watching the man move that he could spring from that chair in a heartbeat if he needed to.

"Haven't you met Jesse Tanner yet?" Ford asked behind them. "He's the sheriff's brother."

Emily spun around, breathing heavily with obvious surprise and displeasure. "What is he doing here?" she demanded, then lowered her voice to add, "Liam needs his rest."

Ford nodded. "The deputy is here to make sure he gets it."

"Deputy?" Emily was visibly trying to calm herself. "I'd like a moment alone with my husband."

"Jesse doesn't leave the room," Ford said. "But don't worry. He won't disturb you."

"On whose orders?"

"Rozalyn's," Ford said, knowing that he carried no weight at all in this matter. But Rozalyn did. She was the man's daughter, his blood, although legally Emily could put up a fight. But it would take time and a lawyer. "She just wants to make sure her father is safe."

"Safe?! He's in a hospital! What is wrong with that girl?" Emily snapped with disgust. "The sheriff told me that she thought she saw someone jump from Lost Creek Falls?" She was shaking her head as if the idea was ludicrous. "You know her mother committed suicide. Jumped from the widow's walk in the attic."

He tried not to show his shock. No wonder Rozalyn had freaked out at the falls like she had.

Emily nodded, obviously pleased that she'd shocked him. "I have to live in that house knowing what that poor deranged woman did just upstairs...."

"You can't get me *near* that attic," Suzanne said, slurring her words.

"The worst part is that this sort of thing runs in Rozalyn's family," Emily said with a shudder. "I'm sure she just imagined seeing someone jump from the falls. It wouldn't be the first time. Her father told me she heard voices and music all the time after her mother's death."

Ford wished now that he'd seen the jumper. He didn't want to agree with this woman that Rozalyn had just imagined the whole thing. "Losing a parent like that has to be a shock," he said, thinking of his own father's quiet death and how it had affected him.

He couldn't imagine what Rozalyn must have gone through after her mother's suicide.

"Rozalyn is unstable. Why else would she think she saw a jumper at the river? Or that Liam was in danger?" Emily demanded.

"I'll leave you alone to visit with your husband,"

Ford said. He glanced in Jesse's direction, their eyes meeting in silent understanding. Nothing could get Jesse Tanner out of that room short of a stretcher.

"I just wanted to tell Liam good night," Emily said and went around to the side of the bed to pat her husband's pale hand. Drew and Suzanne hadn't moved from their spots near the door.

As Ford headed down the hall, he passed Dr. Harris and heard Emily greet the doctor with, "Oh Mark, I'm so worried about Liam." Ford heard the doctor reassuring her in a soft caring tone. "Is there any way you can get that awful man out of Liam's room?"

"I guess the sheriff insisted at the request of the daughter. My hands are tied, Em."

As Ford left the hospital, the sky to the west glittered with lightning. He could practically feel the low rumble of thunder echo in his chest. It wouldn't be long now before all hell broke loose, he thought, thinking of the coming storm—and the one inside him.

ROZ PARKED in front of the house noticing that, while a couple of lights burned inside, Drew's car was gone. Were they still at the hospital?

Roz had hoped everyone had gone to bed. She could feel the approaching storm in the air as she walked quickly up the steps and across the porch. She was relieved that the porch light was on and the front door wasn't locked. She felt a little chilled and couldn't wait to have a hot bath as lightning flickered in the distance, thunder echoing behind it, the night suddenly feeling colder.

She hurried inside, trying to be as quiet as possible in hopes of avoiding running into any of the family again tonight—just in case any were home.

She didn't see anyone as she closed the front door behind her and started up the stairs. From the kitchen came the clatter of pots and pans, but no other sound.

Roz hurried up the stairs, trying not to think about Ford Lancaster. Impossible. If even half of what he'd told her was the truth—

As she passed the second floor, she heard nothing but silence. Was it possible even Suzanne had gone to the hospital? Could she be wrong about the level of their concern for her father?

She *was* tired. Exhausted with worry and from being around these people. Biting her tongue took so much energy. Not that she'd done much tongue biting tonight.

She opened the door to her room, thankful now that it hadn't been changed. It felt like a sanctuary in this house and she needed that right now. She closed the door and caught the scent of chocolate—her one weakness.

In a dish next to her bed were two perfect pieces of her favorite Swiss chocolates—and a note. "I thought you might enjoy these after the day you've had, Drew."

How thoughtful. Roz popped one of the chocolates into her mouth and closed her eyes, letting the rich, smooth delicacy melt on her tongue. "Ahhhhh."

She'd save the other one for after a hot bath.

As she turned, she caught a movement out of the

corner of her eye. Her pulse jumped and she had to stifle a scream.

It was only the curtain billowing in on a gust of wind. Her relief was short-lived. She hadn't left the window open. Maybe Drew had opened it to let in some fresh air. Odd, though, she couldn't imagine anyone doing that with a thunderstorm on the way.

A cold draft of damp air curled around her neck as she went to the window, frowning as she looked down. Past the narrow window ledge was a drop of three stories to the garden below. She glanced up through the limbs of the large tree directly outside her room and caught sight of a dark figure moving along the garden path toward the guest house. Ford?

She started to close the window but stopped as she noticed how close the branches of the tree were to her room. It would be easy for someone to climb the tree and right into her room.

She shook off the thought as she closed the window and locked it. Why would anyone go to the effort, let alone the danger of falling from a rain-slick tree limb to climb in her window? Especially when the window had been closed and locked when she'd left earlier. Hadn't it? It had definitely been closed. She couldn't swear it had been locked though.

She turned to survey the room, her gaze settling on her open suitcase.

Earlier when she'd left, her suitcase hadn't been open on the trunk at the end of her bed.

But it was now.

She stepped to it, seeing at once that the contents had been gone through—and not very neatly—as if the person had been in a hurry. Drew? It seemed unlikely that it had been him. He wouldn't leave her chocolates and a note, and then rummage through her suitcase in such a way that she'd notice. Someone else had been in her room!

Her mouth went dry as she looked around. What had someone been searching for? Had he climbed the tree?

Or just left the window open to make her think the intruder had come from outside the house—rather than from within?

Ford Lancaster looked more than capable of scaling that tree and coming in through her bedroom window. That image tantalized her imagination a little too much and she quickly moved on to other suspects.

Emily was nosey enough that Roz could easily see her going through the suitcase. But she was also cheap enough that she wouldn't leave the window open. Too much heat loss.

Roz sighed. As far as in-house suspects, that left Suzanne. Suzanne didn't seem motivated or sober enough to go through her suitcase let alone open the window to make her think someone had just left moments before Roz arrived.

Roz looked out, thinking of Ford.

That pretty much left Ford. She'd just seen him from the window. He could have scaled down the tree only moments before. That *had* been him she'd seen heading for the guest house, hadn't it? He'd certainly made good time walking back, even though Timber Falls was small and the hospital was only a few blocks away.

But what would Ford have been looking for in her suitcase? What would anyone have been looking for?

She locked the window and froze as she heard a familiar song playing in the room next door, her mother's sewing room. The song was her mother's favorite—and the same song Roz heard in her nightmares.

Heart pounding, she moved across her bedroom and opened the door to peer out. The hallway was empty. She was only imagining the music—just as she had earlier tonight. Just as she had right after her mother's death. Just as she did when she dreamed about her mother's death.

But this time it sounded so real. And this time there was no mistaking where the music was coming from.

She tiptoed down the hallway, stopping at the sewing room door. The knob felt cold to the touch. It turned in her hand and the door swung open.

The room, like her own, was exactly the same as it had been ten years ago. Some of her mother's fabric was still spread out on the cutting table, the scissors lying next to it, as if any moment her mother would pick them up.

The song stopped, and in the silence that followed, she thought she really had imagined it. But then the record began to play again, startling her and she saw why.

Her mother's old automatic phonograph. The single 45 spinning on the turntable. The record scratchy, the speakers tinny sounding.

She stepped into the chilly room, lifted the needle

off the 45 and turned the record player to off. Silence filled the room.

She wasn't going to cry. Wasn't that exactly what someone wanted her to do? Why else had they turned on the phonograph? But how? Wasn't everyone at the hospital?

As she started to turn toward the open doorway to leave, she heard a soft click behind her and froze.

An instant later the phonograph needle began to scratch across the record again.

Chapter Six

As Ford walked to the guest house from the hospital, the town of Timber Falls was quiet and dark as if holding its breath before the next rainstorm hit.

He stopped on the porch, took out his keys and started to unlock the guest house door. He froze, the hair rising on the back of his neck. The door was already open and he had the feeling that whoever had broken in either hadn't been gone long—or was still inside.

He reached into his pocket for his penlight but didn't turn it on as he slowly pushed open the door. It was black inside the guest house except for a sliver of light under his bedroom door. He could hear a faint rustling on the other side.

Cautiously, he moved closer. A floorboard creaked under his shoe. The light under the door went out. He snapped on the penlight and threw open the door just in time to see a dark figure rush out through the patio doors and out into the night.

He gave chase but the intruder was quickly swallowed up by the rainforest. Ford swore under his breath. He couldn't even be sure if it had been a man or a woman. Nor could he make out a footprint in the mossy ground outside.

Closing the patio doors, he found marks where a tool had been used to break the lock. So why had the front door been open? Had someone just wanted him to believe they'd broken in when in truth, the intruder had used a key and not closed the door properly?

He closed the drapes and pulled a chair up under the doorknob of the patio door for the night. He would do the same to the front door when the time came.

As he turned back to the room, he saw that his things had been gone through. His papers were scattered on the floor where they'd been dropped.

Adrenaline shot through him. Where was his laptop computer?

He hurried around the bed, relieved to see it lying next to the bed on the floor. Even before he reached for it, he knew that the disk would be gone.

It was.

He swore again. Whoever had stolen the disk now knew as much about Liam Sawyer's find as Ford did. But then again, whoever had broken in here had already known something or he wouldn't have come here tonight.

Ford mentally kicked himself. He'd provided the thief with the perfect opportunity by staying away so long. But that was the least of his worries. That disk had more than Liam's find on it. If any of that information should get to Rozalyn—

He rubbed his sore shin where she'd kicked him earlier in the garden and thought about, of all things, the kiss.

He'd lied. It hadn't been *nothing*. In fact those few delightful moments in the garden made him curious enough to want to kiss her again. He swore at the thought, reminding himself of the kind of woman Rozalyn Sawyer was. The kind who would risk her life for a phantom stranger at a waterfall.

Just his luck that the one person who actually might be able to help him would be the least predictable and the most honest.

ROZ STOOD, her back to the sewing room as the heart-breakingly familiar record began to play on the phonograph again. A chill skittered across her skin, the tiny hairs on the back of her neck rising. That same song had been playing the day her mother jumped from the fourth floor widow's walk to fall to her death. No one had believed Roz that the song had been playing any more than they believed that she'd heard voices in the attic before her mother was found.

Nor would anyone believe that Roz had turned off the record player.

And that *someone* had turned it back on.

Out of the corner of her eye, she spied her mother's scissors on the cutting table. Holding her breath, she grabbed for the scissors. The instant her hand closed over them, she whirled around, brandishing the sharp weapon.

There wasn't another soul in the room. Just as she knew there wouldn't be. The record whirled on the phonograph. The music filled the room. She was completely alone.

Tears of terror blurred her eyes as she rushed back in, grabbed the cord and jerked the plug from the wall. A final note hung in the air as the needle scratched across the vinyl, the arm dropping away from the record.

She stood over the phonograph, the silence louder and more eerie than the music had been. She stared down at the 45 as if she half expected the record to begin spinning again and the needle to rise and drop to the scratchy vinyl surface.

The scissors clattered to the floor. She grabbed the record from the turntable and began to break it into tiny pieces that fell to the floor like dark confetti until her trembling hands were empty and she ran from the room, slamming the door behind her.

She wanted to keep going, out of this house, out of this town, away from all the painful memories. But she couldn't leave her father. She ran to her bedroom and hurriedly locked the door behind her.

Nor would she be frightened away.

Checking under the bed, in the closet and even behind the shower curtain in the bathroom, she tried to still her panic.

Lightning splintered the sky beyond her window, followed moments later by a deafening boom of thunder. She cried out, backing up against the wall as she watched the sky outside flash with light.

She had to calm down. Someone was trying to scare her and damn but it was working. Exhaustion made her brain foggy. She tried to think, tried to get her composure back. Her mother's spirit hadn't started that phonograph playing. Nor was it the electrical storm or some quirk of nature. Someone had to have rigged the phonograph to keep playing even when she'd turned it off.

Emily! The woman had resented her from the beginning. She definitely didn't want her here. Drew was the only one who seemed to care anything about her.

Roz saw the second piece of chocolate on the plate by her bed and almost dove for it. Once in her mouth, the rich chocolate began to melt, and Roz felt her heart rate drop a little. She would never be able to sleep unless she got a hot bath even as late as it was. She was too worried about her father. Too keyed up over everything.

But she'd also seen too many movies where the heroine foolishly climbed into the tub not realizing the killer was in her bedroom. She double-checked the closet, under the bed and made sure the window was locked, then she barricaded herself in the bathroom after first looking behind the shower curtain again.

The chocolate was starting to take effect. She felt a mellowness wash over her as she turned on the faucet and the large claw-foot tub began to fill.

She could hardly hear the thunder rumbling outside. Without a window, she couldn't see the flashes of lightning. Maybe by the time she was through bathing, the storm would have died down to just rain.

She tried not to worry about her father, praying he would have regained consciousness by morning. She also tried not to think about the phonograph. Or the open window she'd found earlier in her bedroom. Or the fact that someone had gone through her suitcase.

As the tub filled, she opened the bottle of jasmine bubble bath that had been set out for her and poured a large dollop into the water. Drew again?

She yawned, stripped off her clothing and stepped into the tub, groggily sinking neck-deep into the warm water and jasmine-scented bubbles. The water felt like silk as it caressed her skin, warming her to her core. She closed her eyes.

Heaven. She was surprised how drowsy she felt suddenly, and behind her lids, saw a figure in a yellow raincoat running through the golden beams of her highlights and the pouring rain, heading for the brink of a waterfall.

Her eyes flew open. She shoved the image away. She didn't want to think what the sheriff would find at Lost Creek Falls.

As she lay back in the tub, she let herself drift to the soft lap and warm feel of the water, pretending she was supine on a raft under the summer sun, the ocean beneath her the color of Ford's eyes.

Her eyes closed, her lids too heavy to keep open. Ford's image appeared as if conjured up. Those insolent sea-green eyes met hers. His gaze caressed her face, her neck, her—

Her eyes flew open and she sat up, sloshing water in the tub. She looked around the room. His image had been so real that she expected to see Ford standing over her. The room was empty. Of course it was. The door was locked. She must have dozed off. She could have drowned.

"That's enough of that." It seemed to take all her energy to pull herself from the tub, rub herself dry with the towel, don the long white cotton nightgown she'd brought and unlock the bathroom door let alone climb into bed.

As exhausted as she was, she found herself fighting

sleep, afraid to close her eyes for fear of what she might see. Worse, what she might hear—the unbroken favorite 45 playing again on her mother's phonograph in the next room.

She stared hard at the ceiling, willing her lids open. It took all her effort. The old house creaked and groaned. Lightning flashed beyond the window curtains, thunder rattled the glass, echoing like a heartbeat inside her. Roz didn't even remember closing her eyes.

FORD COULDN'T SLEEP. After tossing and turning for a while, he finally gave up. He pulled on only a pair of jeans and padded barefoot into the kitchen to make himself a drink. He could feel the electricity in the air and smell the scent of the approaching rain as he took his glass out to the covered porch.

The wind groaned in the swaying tops of the trees, as lightning cut huge zigzagged seams in the darkness and thunder cracked like a shot overhead. He waited out the storm, restless and edgy.

The first sip of Scotch burned all the way down. Just what he needed. He knew he wouldn't be able to sleep until the storm moved on, until the rain fell in a monotonous downpour.

He looked toward the house, wondering if Rozalyn was asleep. She'd looked exhausted at the hospital. Why wouldn't she be asleep after the night she'd had. He tried not to feel sorry for her. A weird stepfamily. Her father in the hospital in a coma. And maybe even worse, Ford Lancaster dropping into her life. Talk about bad karma.

And there was her past. Her family's history of

instability. He knew how that could haunt a person. It certainly could explain her reaction at Lost Creek Falls tonight. Of course, he hadn't seen a thing. Another sore point between them. Another reason she wouldn't want to trust him. As if she needed any more reasons.

He took another sip of his drink and smiled ruefully. He'd pretty much blown it with her. Except maybe for the kiss. For that moment he'd thought he had her right where he wanted her. She had been responding quite nicely. Until she kicked him.

He shook his head, amazed she'd come back here after her mother had committed suicide in that house. The woman had grit, that was for damned sure. Look at how she'd stood up to Emily and the rest of them. He smiled to himself. *Look how she stood up to you.*

He walked to the edge of the porch railing. This was the last place in the world he wanted to be. Worse, he hated what he was going to have to do. One thing was for certain, he couldn't let Rozalyn find out the truth from whoever had taken the disk. Not before she helped him find whatever it was Liam Sawyer had discovered in the woods before his injury.

Ford glanced toward the main house again. He couldn't see most of the structure because of the trees. But he could see the attic windows clearly. At first he thought he'd just imagined the flicker of light behind one of the windows.

He waited for the light to come on again.

It didn't.

Lightning ripped through the darkness in a blinding flash. A heartbeat later, thunder boomed.

Still no light flickered in the attic. Odd. Maybe he

had just imagined it. Or the glow had been the re-flection of lightning on the windowpane.

He looked down at his glass, surprised it was empty, and went back in to make another drink, trying to convince himself that whatever happened to Roza-lyn Sawyer, she wasn't his responsibility. He would just get what he wanted and get out. Like he always had.

Inside the guest house, he sloshed a little more Scotch into his glass. The screen door banged against the door frame as the storm picked up. The first few drops of rain splattered loudly on the porch roof.

Ford could feel the power of the storm in the cold air blowing in through the screen door. He was al-ready wired but now the night held an odd expecta-tion that made the hair rise on his forearms.

He slipped on athletic shoes and a T-shirt, picked up his drink and went back out on the porch again to watch the storm. Between the crashes of thunder, he could hear the rain pelting the leaves out in the dark-ness as the storm centered itself over the town as if hunkering down for the duration.

He breathed a sigh of relief. Finally. Rain. Won-derful monotonous rain that would let him sleep. He realized he didn't need the Scotch and dumped the contents of his glass over the railing, anxious now for the oblivion of sleep, the one place he might find peace.

But as he turned to go back inside, he made the mistake of glancing toward the house again. This time there was no mistaking the flicker of a flashlight beam behind one of the attic windows. He watched the light bob across the attic and wondered what someone was doing up there. He imagined most of the family agreed with Suzanne; they wouldn't be caught dead up there.

The flashlight went out as a lamp flared in the right-hand corner of the attic. Odd. The person who had turned it on was behind a pillar. He waited for the person to step out.

Instead, the movement came from off to the right. A figure in a long white nightgown appeared as if an apparition. Even from this distance he recognized the hair. Long and strawberry-blond, it floated around her shoulders, shimmering in the lamplight.

She moved to one of the windows at the center of the attic. For the first time he noticed the widow's walk.

His glass slipped from his fingers. He was already running toward the house as Rozalyn Sawyer opened the windows wide and climbed out onto the widow's walk four stories above the ground, the wind whipping the cloth of the white nightgown around her slim body, her strawberry-blond hair now aglow in the light of the storm, as rain fell in large, hard and angry drops from the darkness.

Chapter Seven

Ford let out an oath as he barreled through the dense vegetation of the garden to the back of the house. Above him, Rozalyn balanced on the edge of the widow's walk—just as she had at the falls. The hem of her nightgown snapped in the wind through a curtain of rain.

He didn't dare call to her. Didn't dare draw her attention downward. Running to the back door, he tried the knob, not surprised to find it locked. *Bang on the door. Get someone up there. Quick.*

He rejected the idea as quickly as it had come. The noise alone might cause her to jump. Looking upward, he realized there was only one way to reach her. He'd have to climb the tree next to the house.

The cold soaking rain beat down on him as he quickly began to climb. Lightning fractured the darkness. Thunder detonated overhead.

Climbing a tree in a thunderstorm. *Great, Lancaster.* And all to save a woman who was bound and determined to kill herself. If he lucked out and didn't slip and fall from the wet tree limbs, he'd probably get struck by lightning.

And as if his luck couldn't get any worse, the tree wasn't high enough to take him all the way to the attic. He crawled out on a limb near one of the windows on the third floor. He started to break the window but saw that someone had already broken the lock. A screwdriver lay on the edge of the windowsill out of view from inside.

He took the screwdriver, inserted it between the window and frame in the same grooves made earlier and lifted. The window rose with a groan.

A flash of lightning illuminated a girl's room. Rozalyn's former bedroom?

Still hanging on to the limb, he swung over to the windowsill, then ducking down, dropped into the room with a thud. A cat burglar he wasn't.

On top of the open suitcase on a trunk at the end of the bed was the rust-colored sweater Rozalyn had been wearing earlier. It was her bedroom all right. Except she should have been sacked out, sound asleep. But the bed was empty, the covers thrown back.

He rushed out into the hallway wondering how to get to the attic as he glanced toward the staircase. Not that way. He swung his gaze back down the hallway and felt a chill. There was a dark space between the paneling and wall at the end the hall. A secret door of some kind.

He ran down the hall. Definitely a secret door. A faint light glowed at the top of a set of steep narrow steps that rose upward. On the closest step he saw one small barefoot print in the dust. Rozalyn.

With only a moment's hesitation at the thought of

the door closing behind him and being trapped inside, he scrambled up the steps, hoping he could get out at the top as easily as he'd gotten in.

He hadn't gone far when he heard something that made him miss a step. A shudder tore through him. Cripes, what the hell was that?

But he knew even before he reached the top of the stairs, grateful to see another hidden door—also open, and beyond it the source of the light and the blood-curdling sound.

A small lamp glowed in a corner of the huge attic. Most of the room was filled with antiques that had been piled along one side, leaving the side along the windows open.

His breath caught when he recognized the source of the high-pitched keening. Rozalyn. He followed the horrific sound and her dusty barefooted prints across the attic, drawing up short just behind the widow's walk.

The hair rose on the back of his neck. Rozalyn stood framed against the darkness, her feet balancing on the six-inch wide railing, nothing else but air between her and the ground four stories below. Her head was thrown back, the hideous pain-filled cry emanating from her throat.

"Rozalyn?" he said softly, afraid that he might startle her. He thought of when he'd grabbed her earlier tonight at the waterfall. Unfortunately, he wasn't as close this time.

He took a couple of steps toward her. The old wooden floorboards under him groaned. He froze.

She hadn't moved, hadn't seemed to have heard

him over her cries. Her arms stretched out as if she
planned to do a swan dive off a high board. Her soaking wet nightgown clung to her body, the hem snap-
ping in the wind.

He took another couple of steps toward her, afraid
to say anything this close to her for fear she might
fall. Or jump. Another step or two and he would be
close enough to make a grab for her. But her flesh
would be wet and slick. She'd be damned hard to
hang on to.

The keening sound stopped with a suddenness that
rattled him. The deathly silence that followed was almost more frightening. Suddenly her head jerked to
one side as if she heard something on the wind.

His breath caught in his throat as she turned her
head slowly toward him. He feared seeing him would
frighten her.

Her eyes. Oh God, her eyes.

He swore under his breath and grabbed for her.

The moment his fingers clamped over her wrist, she
blinked, the glazed eyes fighting to focus on him. She
let out a cry of alarm, swaying on the railing. Her
wrist was slick from the rain. He got his arm around
her waist as she tried to pull away, seeming confused,
frightened, disoriented.

She looked down then at the ground far below her
and let out a startled cry, staggering backward. He
caught her in his arms and carried her away from the
widow's walk and the four-story drop back into the
attic.

"Where is she?" Rozalyn cried the moment he set
her down a safe distance from the windows. She sunk

to the floor as if her legs wouldn't hold her. She was trembling and her eyes were still glassy. "Where is she?"

His heart quickened.

She looked past him as if she thought there was someone else in the attic with them. "Didn't you hear her?"

"Who?" he asked on a breath.

"My mother. She was calling me." Her voice broke with emotion as she glanced toward the widow's walk and shuddered, tears welling in her eyes. "Tell me you heard her," she said in a whisper, looking up at him as if she was depending on him.

You're looking at the wrong guy, he thought. "Sorry."

"I don't understand—" A sob broke from her.

"You were walking in your sleep. I have a little sister who does the same thing." He couldn't get the frightening image of her eyes from his mind. She'd looked blind, lost in another world miles away.

"Sleepwalking?" She was trembling so hard he could practically hear her teeth chatter. He dragged a worn quilt from a pile on one of the ornate antique tables and draped it around her.

"Lisa usually walked during a bad dream." He hoped that was all it was in Rozalyn's case.

"I heard something."

Just like she'd seen something earlier at the waterfall? "Old houses make strange noises sometimes—"

"It wasn't the house." She shuddered. "My mother. She was calling me, *to help her.*" Eyes swimming in tears, she glanced toward the widow's walk where her mother had committed suicide. Her face crumpled. "What was I doing out there?"

He wished he knew. "I'm sure it was just a bad dream," he said, not sure of that at all. If anything, it was more like a nightmare since something had gotten her to climb out onto the railing of that widow's walk.

She looked around again, clearly not so sure now, still seeming disoriented. "It was so real," she whispered.

"Dreams can be like that," he said softly and brushed a lock of wet hair back from her cheek. Just before her brown eyes boiled over with tears again, he got a good look at them. "What are you on?"

"What?" She wiped at her tears, staring up at him.

"Drugs, what did you take?"

"Nothing. I don't take drugs."

"Not even something to sleep?"

She shook her head, quickly stopping the motion, eyes closing tightly as if the movement had made her sick.

"You're coming with me." He pulled her to her feet. She swayed, obviously woozy. He expected her to put up a fight but without a word she let him carry her to the paneled opening and the hidden staircase.

She was trembling, from the cold, fear and whatever drug dulled her eyes as he helped her descend the narrow steps. Then he carried her to her bedroom.

"We have to get you into something dry," he said quietly as he closed the door behind them. When he turned back to her, she had slumped on the edge of the bed clutching the quilt as if lost.

He went into the bathroom, came back with a couple of large towels and toweled the rainwater from her hair. He was tempted to get her into the bathtub but it would take too long to fill. He had a shower in the guest house. All he had to do was get her there.

He found clothing, hiking boots, her toothbrush and stuffed everything into a pillowcase from the bed. He handed it to her, swept her up again and quietly carried her down the stairs, out the back door and through the rain and garden to the guest house.

Once inside, he took her into the bathroom. She sat on the toilet seat still wrapped in the quilt as he turned on the shower. Steam filled the room quickly and, when he was sure it was warm enough, he gently pulled her to her feet and slipped the quilt off her shoulders.

The nightgown clung to her like a second skin. He sucked in a breath at the sight of her body flushed under the thin white fabric.

"Damn," he breathed. She was beautiful, her skin lightly freckled and pale, her breasts full and round, her nipples dark and hard against the wet cotton. She had a slim waist, a flat stomach and a small mound of strawberry-blond hair at the vee between her legs.

She took his breath away.

"Rozalyn," he said softly as he looked into her dark eyes. She trembled, still looking dazed, and he couldn't be sure if it was because of the drug she'd ingested or hypothermia setting in. He had to get her warmed up and straightened out. "I'm going to take off your wet nightgown."

She didn't resist, didn't speak or even blink as he pulled the nightgown up over her head and drew her toward the shower. She stumbled and leaned into him as if her legs still would not hold her.

Kicking off his shoes, still in his jeans and T-shirt, he stepped into the shower with her, holding her as the warm water cascaded over her naked body. She wrapped her arms around his neck, her face against his chest, and he held her to him and thought about baseball rather than the naked woman in his arms.

After a few minutes, her trembling slowed. Warm steam filled the small bathroom like thick warm fog. He stood with her until they'd emptied the hot water tank, until her skin was bright pink.

She seemed stronger, more steady once they were out of the shower as if shedding the effects of the drug—if not the horror of what could have happened up there on the widow's walk.

Mentally reciting major league statistics, he quickly toweled her dry and pulled one of his dry T-shirts over her head. It was large enough that it dropped to below her knees, covering her glorious body.

Wrapping her in a dry quilt from the bed, he carried her to the living room couch where he deposited her while he went into the bedroom to change into dry clothes himself. He needed a drink. Desperately.

When he came back out, she looked up. She hadn't said a word in the shower or out. She looked a hundred percent better. "I know what you're thinking."

"I doubt that," he said softly.

"You think I went up there to jump," she said in a whisper.

He shook his head. "I think someone drugged you and somehow tricked you into going up to the attic and getting on that widow's walk."

"How is that possible?"

"I don't know. You appeared to be in a hypnotic state. At first I thought you were walking in your sleep. Until I got a good look at your pupils."

"My mother jumped to her death from that same widow's walk," she said shakily.

He nodded.

"Don't you think it's a little strange that I would go up there like I did and—" Her voice broke.

"You weren't up there trying to kill yourself or you would have jumped before I got to you," he said.

She didn't look so sure about that. "How *did* you happen to see me in the attic? I don't remember anything except being really drowsy and going to bed."

He sighed. "I was out on the guest house porch waiting for the storm when I saw a light in one of the attic windows. Then I saw you. I climbed the tree beside the house, went through your bedroom and up those stairs hidden in the wall."

"The door was open?" she asked surprised.

He nodded. "Your bare footprints were in the dust so I knew that was the way you'd gone up." Now that he thought about it, there were no other footprints.

"You climbed the tree outside my bedroom?" Her cheeks flushed.

He wondered why she was blushing. "The lock

was already broken. There was a screwdriver on the ledge where someone had pried open the window before I came along.''

''Well, whatever made me go up there, thank you for—'' she waved a hand through the air, her gaze shifting toward the bathroom, her cheeks in high color ''—for saving me.''

He met her gaze and didn't like what he saw. She thought he was some kind of hero. Far from it. ''You would have awakened and climbed down if I hadn't shown up.''

She gave him a look that said they both knew better than that.

''After you came back from the hospital, what did you have to drink?'' he asked.

She frowned. ''Nothing. I had a couple of Swiss chocolates—''

''Ones you brought with you?''

She shook her head slowly. ''No, they were in a dish beside the bed with a note from Drew.''

He swore under his breath. ''I didn't see a note when I was looking for a change of clothing for you. Are you sure Drew left the chocolates?''

''No. His name was on the note but I wouldn't know his handwriting.'' She stared at him as if just starting to comprehend what he was saying. ''You think there was something in the chocolates? You can't think that someone in the house put drugs in—''

''Any member of *that* family is capable, Emily included. They all had access to your room and someone had either gone in your bedroom window or wanted you to believe they had.''

She bit her lower lip. ''That's what I thought when I returned from the hospital to find the window open. Someone had gone through my suitcase.'' She looked at him. ''You don't think I'm crazy?''

''I'm not saying that.'' He smiled. ''You want some coffee?''

She shook her head. ''I want to sleep for a week.''

Her brown eyes were clearer, the effects of the drug wearing off. He went to the bar and sloshed some Scotch into a glass. He pressed it into her hand. ''Just a sip.''

She stared down at it, lifted the glass to her lips, drank a little and made a face.

He smiled at her. ''It's an acquired taste.''

''Not one I care to acquire,'' she said and handed him back the glass.

He drained what little was left and looked down at her. She looked as if she'd been dragged through the wringer. Right now she was giving him one of her narrowed-eye looks. He could almost hear the wheels turning in her head. She was trying to figure him out, no doubt finally realizing that he might have an ulterior motive for everything he'd been doing. He smiled to himself, liking the fact that the woman was sharp.

''Why are you being so nice to me?'' she asked.

''What makes you think I'm not always nice?''

''I'm serious.''

''I can see that.''

She studied him. He tried not to flinch.

"I don't mean to sound unappreciative but...I just feel like there might be some reason you keep saving me."

"Just my bad luck at being in the wrong place at the wrong time," he said.

"Or my good luck?"

He wanted to tell her that his coming into her life would be considered anything but good luck. But hell, that would be counterproductive to getting what he wanted now, wouldn't it?

"You can have the bed," he said and turned his back to walk down the short hall to the linen closet where he took out bedding. "I'll take the couch."

ROZ COULDN'T believe it. Damn, if she wasn't careful she was going to start trusting him. She stared after the man, reminding herself who he was. Ford Lancaster. But how could everything that had happened tonight *not* change her original opinion of him?

He'd written that article years ago and he'd had his reason for wanting to hurt his father. Now he was trying to make up for what he'd done by helping her and her father.

So why was something still niggling at her, something that warned her not to be taken in by him no matter how kind or caring he appeared to be?

She looked into those pale green eyes as he returned to the room and felt a slight tremor. "You aren't just trying to get me to lower my defenses by being nice to me, are you?"

His smile was disarming. "You're too smart for that."

She gave him a wary look as he put the bedding on the couch next to her and felt a moment's alarm.

He chuckled. "Rozalyn, sex is the last thing on my mind right now."

Really? She wished *she* could say that. She didn't like the feeling just looking into his eyes gave her. She thought about his arms around her in the shower, her naked body pressed against—

"You should try to get some sleep," he said. "We can talk about my plans to get you to lower your defenses in the morning."

He was trying to make light of it but was it possible he was feeling what she was? Obviously not. She got to her feet. "Thank you. For everything tonight."

He smiled at that. "You make it sound like I took you on a date."

Why did he have to make it so hard to thank him?

"Before our date ends, there's something I need you to do." He went into the kitchen and came back with a paper cup. He handed it to her. "Give me a sample."

"You aren't serious."

"Humor me, okay? It's not like I asked you to get naked again." His gaze met hers. "Or have sex with me."

She felt herself flush in spite of the fact that he was baiting her. "You don't take compliments well."

He raised a brow obviously finding humor in that. "I've had so few I'm at a loss as to how to take them."

"Are you ever serious?"

"I'm serious right now," he said, his pale aqua

gaze boring into hers. He pushed the paper cup at her. "Just leave it beside the sink."

She thought of him in the shower with her, how strong and solid and comforting he'd been. A different man than the one standing in front of her now. Or was that just what he wanted her to believe? Her defenses had definitely been down when they'd been in the shower together. If he had wanted to take advantage of her, he could have and she sensed he'd known it. So why hadn't he?

Was it possible he really was in Timber Falls to make amends for what he did to her father—and his own?

She pushed aside her misgivings. The man had saved her life and she was here with him now, planning to spend the rest of the night under the same roof, just feet from him.

"I didn't bring you out here to jump your bones, if that's what you're worried about," he said, looking amused.

"It never crossed my mind."

"Right." The look in his eyes curled her toes as he smiled lazily at her. "Just get some rest, okay?"

"You're an impossible man, you know that?" she said.

"It's been pointed out to me on numerous occasions."

"I'm sure it has." She started toward the bedroom.

"I need to do a couple of things early in the morning. I'm sure you'll want to go see your father before we head out into the woods. Why don't I meet you back here at, say, nine o'clock?"

She turned to look at him, wondering what he had to do in the morning. "Okay."

His back was to her as he started to make a bed on the couch for himself.

"See you in the morning," she said to his broad back, then turned, noticing that a chair had been wedged under the knob of the patio door in the bedroom. "What's with the chair under the doorknob?"

Ford had forgotten for a moment about the break-in. He turned to find her standing in the doorway and realized that wasn't all he'd forgotten. "I had an uninvited visitor earlier. Don't worry, he won't be back. The chair is just a precaution."

"Did he take anything?"

For just a moment, he actually thought about telling her the truth. "No. I guess he must have been looking for something valuable."

"Or something about my father's find," she said quietly. "You think it was the person who attacked my father?" If she hadn't been scared before, she was now. But he couldn't tell if it was for herself or her father. He suspected it was the latter. "We have to find whatever this person is after," she said with brave determination. "My father won't be safe until we do."

We. Ford nodded, torn between his relief and his guilt. Wasn't this exactly what he'd hoped for? She knew her father—and the area—better than he did. If he could just keep her alive, she might prove invaluable.

Yep, he had her right where he wanted her.

Now if he just didn't screw things up—

He stepped to her, thinking about nothing but the fear in her dark eyes and the slight tremble of her lips as her words died off. He hadn't planned to take her in his arms, let alone kiss her.

But she felt so right as his arms closed around her and the soft curves of her body pressed into him. When she looked up and met his gaze, all he could think about was her lush mouth, the feel of her lips, the taste of her.

He lowered his mouth, brushed his lips over hers, a quiver of desire quaking through him. She pushed herself up on tiptoes and kissed him tenderly, a sigh escaping her lips.

All his restraint from earlier in the shower evaporated in an instant as she drew back to look into his eyes. He dropped his mouth to hers, dragging her closer, crushing her to him as he kissed her with a passion that he hadn't known he possessed.

How he wanted her, needed her. The thought left him feeling like he'd been dunked in a bucket of ice water.

He pushed himself back from her. Damn, but he *was* going to screw this up, maybe already had. He could hear his pulse thundering in his ears as he tried to catch his breath and get his equilibrium again. "I'm sorry, I didn't mean to—I…"

She looked as shaken and stunned as he felt as she stumbled back, away from him. She touched her tongue to her upper lip and took a ragged breath. "Good night," she said, looking a little sheepish as she closed the bedroom door.

"Good night." He smiled to himself as he heard

her lock the door. Did she think he would force himself on her? If he had wanted her, he could have taken her earlier in the shower. And without even trying. Or taken her a few moments ago with only a little effort.

No, if they ever made love, it would be with a lot more than just her consent. She'd have to want him as badly as he did her, which was saying a lot.

He chuckled ruefully at the odds of that happening. Sure she'd kissed him back. And it wouldn't be a kiss he'd soon forget. But he knew it had been a kiss born of gratitude. He didn't kid himself about that. He hadn't begun to chip away at her reserve let alone get her to lower her defenses.

But the idea held great appeal. Much more than it should have. He wanted her. Worse, he wanted her to want him with the same fervor. What the hell was wrong with him? He didn't need this, didn't want this.

Lie to everyone else, but don't start lying to yourself, Lancaster. You kissed her because you're starting to feel something for her.

He scoffed at the idea as he walked into the kitchen. He was too smart to fall for Liam Sawyer's daughter. Cripes, how foolish would that be?

No, it was just physical. Nothing more.

He started to pour himself a drink but changed his mind. Now, more than ever he needed his senses about him.

The rain was falling, a hypnotic shower that drummed softly on the roof. He went back into the living room and sprawled on the couch but he knew he wasn't going to be able to sleep.

He closed his eyes, listening to the downpour, thinking about the kiss, angry with himself not only for initiating it but for enjoying it so much.

What kind of fool was he? When she found out the truth about him, she would have nothing to do with him. Worse, if he wasn't careful, he would lose his focus, forget why he was here, forget what really mattered.

But even as he thought it, he remembered the way she'd felt in his arms. Soft. Lush. Amazing...

His eyes flew open and he sat up with a start. The light in the attic. The first one he'd seen had been a flashlight beam. But later when he'd spotted Roz—

He scrubbed his hands over his face and looked toward the closed bedroom door. Rozalyn hadn't had a flashlight. The light had been coming from a lamp as she moved across to the balcony. That meant— The person with the flashlight had turned on the lamp and then...

Rozalyn had been right about one thing, she hadn't been alone in the attic. Someone had been up there. Waiting for her.

He fell back on the couch, but sleep was now out of the question. Someone had drugged Rozalyn tonight, sure as hell. The urine sample would give him an idea of what drug was used once he had it tested. But how did that person get her up to the attic and trick her into climbing out onto the widow's walk where her mother had committed suicide?

And was it just to mess with her mind?

Or to kill her?

One disturbing thought kept him awake long into

the rainy night. Rozalyn Sawyer wasn't safe. Not in that house. Not in Timber Falls. Maybe not anywhere.

And he feared he knew the reason.

Bones.

Chapter Eight

Roz woke to the sun. Outside the patio doors was one of Oregon's famous sunshowers complete with a double rainbow. The storm had passed, leaving the sky clear, sunshine spilling down through the trees like a sign from heaven.

Her father was going to come out of his coma.

She and Ford would find whatever her father had discovered and who had tried to kill him…if someone really had tried. She shuddered at the thought. But Ford believed it so strongly, how could she not?

She got up and showered, reminded of Ford and the night before, the two of them in this shower together. Her cheeks flamed at the memory—including the kiss! Was he still in the next room sleeping or had he already gone out on those errands he had to run?

She promised herself she would keep him at arm's length. No more mistakes like the one last night. If he hadn't stopped the kiss when he had—

She shoved away the thought. The two of them would find out the truth about her father's fall, but there was no way she was lowering her defenses around Ford Lancaster again. He might be attractive to look at but he was dangerous. That was probably what attracted her. She had always picked boring men, safe men. Men she could never get serious about.

She glanced at the closed door, imagining the man behind it. Ford Lancaster was nothing like those men and that's what scared her. With Ford, it would be all or nothing. Total surrender.

As she dumped out the clothes he'd put in the pillowcase for her last night, she was touched again by his kindness. It made her feel a little guilty for still having misgivings about his motivations.

He'd saved her life last night on the widow's walk. Had she just been sleepwalking or was he right? Was it possible someone had put drugs in the chocolates? Drugged or asleep, why would she follow her mother's voice to the attic?

She remembered her mother's favorite record playing on the old phonograph. She would rather believe it was just a short in the wiring. Or a peculiarity of the electrical storm. What she didn't want to believe was that someone in this house actually wanted to hurt her. Even kill her.

And not necessarily someone in the house, she thought, remembering what Ford had said about finding a screwdriver on the ledge outside her window.

She shook her head, as confused as she'd been when she'd awakened to find herself standing on the widow's walk railing about to— About to what? Not jump. No, she would never have done that. Would she have?

Didn't she once read that people often walked in their sleep when they were under a great deal of stress?

Except Ford is convinced you were drugged.

If she had been, she didn't feel any aftereffects. In fact, she was surprised how good she felt. It was as if this was the first good night's sleep she'd had in years. She could only hope her father had also had a good night's rest and was better this morning.

As she finished dressing, the only things she couldn't find were her shoes. She was sure she'd seen her hiking boots here last night. Hadn't she seen Ford dump them out of the pillowcase?

She looked around the room. When she was a teenager, she and Charity had sleepovers in the small guest house. They had stayed up half the night giggling and talking about boys. Of course Charity only talked about Mitch, but Roz would imagine a stranger, some white knight she had yet to meet, who would ride in and carry her away on his trusty steed.

She thought of the man sleeping on the couch in the room beyond the door. No Sir Lancelot that one. Oh, he'd sweep her off her feet, carry her away on his trusty steed, then drop her off without ceremony while she watched him ride into the sunset.

The problem was, he was starting to look like a knight to her. One more heroic act and she'd be a goner.

She thought of how he'd behaved in the shower. She'd been stark naked with the man and he'd been the perfect gentleman.

But that kiss just before she'd gone to bed had been

anything but gentlemanly. She felt her face flame. He'd aroused more than just sexual feelings. His tenderness in the shower coupled with saving her life had drawn her in like a lasso.

She reminded herself that he'd been the one who'd stopped the kiss. Put a halt to what was bound to have happened after the kiss.

Was it possible he had no interest in her other than to keep her alive so she could help him find whatever her father had discovered in the woods?

Well, he'd missed his chance last night.

So why did she feel like she'd missed hers, too?

Because no man had ever stirred these kinds of feelings in her.

It's just gratitude, she told herself as she made the bed and remembered where she'd last seen her hiking boots. Ford had taken them out of the pillowcase and put them down beside the couch.

She moved to the bedroom door and opened it a crack. If he was still here, she didn't want to wake him. And if he was already gone—

He was still here. He lay on the couch, head back, lips parted, snoring lightly. She couldn't help smiling. Something about him snoring made him more human.

And there in front of the couch were the toes of her boots peeking out from under the quilt spread over him.

She tiptoed closer, leaning down to inch toward her boots, enjoying watching him sleep. He looked vulnerable asleep, and the sight touched something deep inside her.

She dropped to her hands and knees and had just reached out for her boots when he let out a sigh and rolled over onto his side, his face just inches from hers. She snagged hold of her boots and slowly slid them toward her.

She was close enough she could see his lashes, black against his skin. His stubborn jawline was dark with stubble and looked rough to the touch. She fought the urge to cup his cheek in her hand, remembering the rough feel of his beard last night when he'd kissed her.

He sighed again, his lashes fluttered, then his lips turned up at the corners in a slow, sexy smile. She felt her heart kick up a beat. She drew her boots to her and slipped back from him. Terrified by the feelings he evoked in her.

Even if everything he'd told her was the truth, he was a disagreeable man, egotistical and self-righteous and impossible. And yet for a startling moment, she had the strongest urge to cup his face in her palms, to press her lips against his, to be a part of that smile. This time it would end in more than a kiss.

Crazy. She was crazy. Maybe she *had* gone up to the attic last night to jump. Maybe she'd been stone-cold sober and awake.

She took one last look at him before retreating out the door into the sunshine. Her heart was pounding and she felt light-headed as she cut through the garden and around the side of the house to her SUV. Then impulsively, as it was such a nice day, she decided to walk to the hospital.

FORD CRACKED one eyelid open as he heard the door close and smiled to himself. For a moment there, he'd thought she was going to kiss him. He'd held his breath, willing himself not to move, not to think about closing her in his arms. He could still smell her scent in the air as he rolled over onto his back and stared up at the ceiling. Damn, he was going to have to take a cold shower. An ice-cold one.

You're enjoying this way too much.

He smiled at that thought. Hell, yes.

It struck him that he wanted her to like him.

He groaned at the thought. "Let's not lose sight of what's at stake here, all right?" he said to himself as he threw back the quilt. "Eventually she's going to find out the truth and you're going to be a bastard again."

So true. He headed for the shower, unable not to remember the night before and the naked woman he'd held in his arms as the warm water cascaded over her skin. He turned the water on cold and threw himself under the icy spray.

He'd just gotten out and dressed when he heard a knock at the door. He thought about ignoring it but whoever it was knew he was in. His pickup was parked right outside.

He opened the door, disappointed to find Drew Lane standing there. He'd rather hoped that Rozalyn had come back to wake him with that kiss.

"Mother thought you might like to join us for breakfast," Drew said as he tried to see past Ford into the room. "Unless you have other plans. Then we're all going to the hospital to see how Liam is doing.''

Obviously Drew had discovered Rozalyn wasn't in her bedroom and thought she might be here. "Please give my apologies to your mother but I do have other plans."

Drew glanced at Ford's still damp dark hair. "Mother will be disappointed," he said, sounding angry.

"Tell her thanks for the invite. Maybe some other time." Ford closed the door and watched with too much satisfaction as Drew scowled and turned to head back through the garden to the house.

Ford reminded himself that if he was right, someone had drugged Rozalyn last night and got her up on that widow's walk railing. That someone could have been Drew Lane. But now wasn't the time to confront him about the chocolates. First Ford had to be sure they'd been drugged.

He hoped Drew would think that Rozalyn was under his watchful eye—if not in his bed. Both were a lie. But then, Drew didn't know that, did he?

As Ford left the house, he thought about what else? Rozalyn Sawyer. What if she really had been at the top of that waterfall last night to jump? What if she hadn't been sleepwalking or drugged? What if she was more damaged by her mother's death than even he was by his father's?

Then the urine sample he had sealed in a container on the seat beside him wouldn't show any drugs, he thought as he drove to the lab and dropped it off. The lab tech put a rush on it for the hundred-dollar incentive Ford offered. He left his cell phone number and the tech promised to get back to him as soon as possible.

Ford picked up three egg-muffin specials at Betty's Café and washed down one on his way to the hospital with one of the two coffees he'd purchased.

A different nurse was at the desk.

"Any change in Liam Sawyer's condition?" he asked.

"The same," she said as he headed down the hall to Liam's room. As far as he could tell, Liam was the hospital's only patient.

From the doorway he saw Rozalyn beside her father's bed, holding his hand, her head bent toward him, talking quietly. Ford motioned to Jesse to come out.

"Hey, breakfast," the deputy said. "Thanks, man." He snarfed down the egg and ham muffins and gulped the coffee Ford had brought him.

"I thought you might need a break," Ford said.

"A short one," Jesse agreed and grinned before sprinting down the hall to the men's lavatory.

Ford stood outside the hospital room door, watching Rozalyn with her father, touched by her tenderness, worried what it would do to her to lose another parent now. He cursed himself as he realized he liked her more all the time and didn't want to see her hurt.

But she would be hurt, he reminded himself.

Jesse returned, his face washed shiny, his long hair wet and tied back again in a ponytail.

"I'm not sure how long I'll be gone today," Ford said.

"No problem. Everything's cool here. Mitch said

he'd stop by to relieve me later. Thanks for break-fast.'' He slipped back into the hospital room. Roza-lyn didn't seem to notice.

Ford left, reminding himself that it was just a mat-ter of time before Rozalyn learned the truth about him—even if the thief who took the computer disk didn't rat him out.

And then there would be no convincing her that he wasn't everything she thought he was.

He just hoped to hell he knew what he was doing. A lot was riding on this. He slid behind the wheel of his pickup and started the engine. He'd better quit thinking about Rozalyn Sawyer and go to work.

But first he had to find out if what he feared about her just might be true.

CHARITY HAD just taken a bite of her banana cream pie when she heard the bell tinkle over the front door of Betty's Café. She closed her eyes. For months now, whenever she ate something rich and wonderful and closed her eyes, she had visions of Sheriff Mitch Tan-ner. Lately, he was always dressed in a tuxedo and—be still her racing heart—he was standing in front of an altar at the church and he was looking at her, smil-ing, as if he loved her more than even he could imag-ine.

''Morning, Charity,'' Mitch said, taking his usual stool next to her.

She opened her eyes and turned to smile at him. ''Good morning, Sheriff.'' Mitch seemed to think he still had a chance of remaining a bachelor. Men could be such fools.

"I saw the paper this morning," he said after Betty slid a cup of coffee and a slice of banana cream pie in front of him without a word and took off as if she knew all hell was going to break loose any moment. Betty knew the two of them well—and had seen today's *Timber Falls Courier*.

Plus Mitch had a copy of the newspaper gripped in his right hand. "Charity," he said under his breath. "I thought I warned you about printing anything that could get you killed."

She looked over at him in surprise. "You think it's that good?"

He groaned. "Do you have a death wish, woman?"

"You said yourself we might never know the truth about the kidnapping unless we rattle a few cages," she whispered back.

"I believe you just misquoted me," he said through gritted teeth. "I said we might never know the truth. Period. The cage rattling was all yours."

"I stand corrected." She smiled at him. "The banana cream pie is amazing this morning." She took another bite and licked her lips.

His dark eyes softened as he watched her, desire sparking in them. Finally, he shook his head as if at something he just couldn't believe. "What am I going to do with you?"

"Oh, I have some great ideas."

"I'm sure you do." He picked up his fork and took a bite of his pie. "I think you'd better get your Aunt Florie to come stay with you until this blows over."

Oh no, they'd been here before. "Not Florie. Look what happened last time."

Last time Mitch had not only had her Aunt Florie staying with her, but also a deputy, and she'd still been abducted and almost killed.

"You're right," he said. "Protecting you from yourself is impossible."

"There is only one man who can protect me," she said and took a forkful of pie, closing her eyes, waiting to see that image of Mitch in the tux. She opened her eyes and winked at him.

"Don't start," Mitch said but there was no humor in his tone.

She took another bite of pie, closed her eyes and saw Mitch at the altar again. She did love him in a tux.

When she opened her eyes he was studying her as if he wondered where she'd gone and what she'd seen behind those closed eyelids. *If he only knew.*

"I know what you're thinking," she said.

"Do you?" he asked, sounding as if he hoped that wasn't the case.

"I'm a journalist. It's like a degree in human nature."

He rolled his eyes. "You have a degree in nosy is all."

She shrugged and smiled. "You might be surprised." She picked up her fork and took a bite of her pie, closing her eyes, waiting for that image of Mitch in the tux.

"I think you should move in with me."

Her eyes flew open. "You're that worried about Wade?"

"I wasn't thinking about Wade."

She cocked her head at him, her heart hammering in her chest. "What exactly are you proposing, Mitch Tanner?"

His dark gaze held hers. He looked nervous as hell. "I think…I think we should be together right now."

Easy, heart. Okay, it was progress. Just not the progress she'd hoped for. A date and he thought they should move in together?

"You're saying you want to take this to the next step or that you're just trying to protect me?" she asked carefully, trying not to start cheering wildly.

He looked around the café. No one was sitting close by but still he seemed to have trouble saying the words. "All I think about is kissing you," he whispered. "It's driving me crazy. I want to make love to you. In a bed. And I don't want to leave afterward and go home. I want you there when I wake up in the morning and when I go to bed at night."

She couldn't catch her breath. How many years had she wished he'd say those words, dreamed he would, waited for him to?

There was just one problem. She wanted to do this right. She came from a family of alternative thinkers, a hippie mom, a fortune-telling aunt, two sisters who spent more time moving in and out of apartments with different boyfriends than Mayflower movers.

But just the thought of going to bed and waking up in Mitch's arms was almost more than she could take. Tears stung her eyes. "Could you be a little more specific?"

He looked past her. "Here comes Roz," he said,

sounding relieved. "I have to go anyway. We'll talk later."

She wanted to scream no! "Aren't you even going to finish your pie?" she asked, afraid she'd only dreamed this conversation.

"No, but I'm sure you won't let it go to waste." Then he did something so out of character it left her speechless—a natural occurrence in its own right. He bent close and kissed her. A quick kiss but right on the lips and then he was gone, saying hello to Roz on his way out.

Charity stared after him, in surprise and delight. She really was making progress with that man. Who would have guessed after all these years?

Her gaze shifted to her old friend. "Roz," she cried, jumping up from the stool and rushing to give her a hug. She would see Mitch later and with a lot of luck, he would finally get up the guts to say the "M" word: marriage.

FORD LANCASTER worked his way down the embankment at Lost Creek Falls, telling himself he was crazier than Rozalyn Sawyer—which was saying a lot.

The slope was treacherous, steep and slippery with moss and spray from the waterfall. He clung to rocks and tree limbs and did his best to keep his feet under him. To make matters worse, he was quickly soaked to the skin from the spray.

He slid down the last few feet to the creek bottom and stood for a moment looking back up at the waterfall—and the huge rock at the top where he'd first met Rozalyn the night before. Just seeing how far up it was made him dizzy and sick to his stomach. If she had fallen·or been pushed—

He didn't even want to think about that. Maybe he hadn't rescued her, hadn't saved her life. Maybe she would have kept her footing and not fallen from the top of the waterfall—let alone jumped. Maybe she wouldn't have done a swan dive off the widow's walk railing last night, either.

But that was why he was here, wasn't it? He told himself he just didn't know and if there was one thing he hated, it was not being one hundred percent certain. It's why he'd become a scientist.

Next to him the water churned and splashed over the rocks, roaring on down the narrow canyon. He stared into the deep green holes as he walked from the base of the waterfall downstream. He was looking for a yellow raincoat, one he didn't expect to find. How crazy was that?

He shook his head, disgusted with himself. He had better things to do and little time. But he wanted desperately to believe her. That was the bottom line, wasn't it? He wanted to believe a woman who didn't believe a word that came out of his mouth—and shouldn't. If he wasn't crazy, he damned sure was some kind of fool.

He moved along the slick moss-covered wet rocks, following the creek as it cut down through the gorge. He told himself he wouldn't be here if it hadn't been for that detour sign. This morning he'd checked. There was only one road off the highway and that came to a dead end here at the falls. He'd called the road department as well.

No mistake. Whoever had put that detour sign there hadn't been authorized to do so.

No, he thought, the person who'd put it there had wanted to get someone to turn off to the falls last night.

Him? Or Rozalyn? There hadn't been anyone else on the highway and with the pouring rain and the lack of traffic this time of year, Ford didn't think it was just an idle prank. Someone had known they would be driving up this way last night and had been waiting for them.

Except he didn't think the detour sign had been put there for him. That meant someone had wanted Rozalyn to see a suicide from the top of the waterfall. And it was too much of a coincidence that Rozalyn's mother had also jumped to her death.

It was a wild theory given he had no proof. Especially for a scientist who operated on fact. Ford prided himself on only believing in things he could see and prove.

But dammit, he'd seen a detour sign in the middle of that highway last night. That's why he'd turned off onto the dead-end road. And that's why Rozalyn had followed him. Unfortunately, she'd been the only one to see someone jump from the falls. Because he'd already turned around and was leaving the waterfall parking lot last night. He shouldn't have seen anything. If he hadn't just happened to look in his side mirror—

Around several bends in the creek, the falls became

only a dull roar in the distance. The water slowed, pooling and circling in the rocks. He was no longer looking for just a yellow raincoat anymore. He was looking for a body. If there had been a detour sign, then there'd been a jumper and that meant there was a body down here somewhere.

And that meant that Rozalyn hadn't imagined it.

He turned another bend, not sure how far he'd gone when he caught a glimpse of something that stopped his heart dead. He swore, slipping and almost falling as he stumbled forward. No yellow raincoat. No, not even close.

In a narrow space between two large rocks were wedged the fingers of a slim hand, the nails painted bright red.

Chapter Nine

Roz hugged Charity and they started chattering as if they'd seen each other only yesterday rather than several months before.

"Let's go sit in a booth," Charity suggested, grabbing a piece of half-eaten banana cream pie and her diet cola. She didn't look any different than she had the last time Roz had seen her in Seattle a few years ago. Except she seemed to glow with happiness.

Roz hadn't missed that kiss the sheriff had given Charity. "I see some things haven't changed," she said as they slid into a booth.

Charity grinned. "Can you believe it? I might convince Mitch that I'm the only woman for him yet." She sobered and reached across the table to clutch her hand. "Oh, Roz, I was so sorry to hear about your dad."

Roz had forgotten how fast news traveled in Timber Falls. "He's going to come out of the coma and be all right."

"Of course he is," Charity agreed. "I'm sure he is just so glad you're here. Just as I am. The last time I saw your dad was a few weeks ago when I accosted him on the street. This black pickup had been following me and your dad was driving a black pickup—''

"Someone was following you?"

Charity waved that off. "Long story. Anyway, it wasn't the same black pickup obviously. Rather embarrassing since your dad's new wife was with him."

"So you met Emily." She didn't have to ask Charity what she thought; she knew her friend too well.

Betty came over to say hello and take Roz's order and then they were finally alone again.

"What's this I hear about Ford Lancaster staying at your guest house?" Charity whispered.

"It's a long story." She felt her cheeks flush.

"A long story I'm going to have to hear some time. He really is good-looking, isn't he? I saw him when he was in town a couple of weeks ago. Didn't Emily know who he was?"

"She says she didn't." Roz frowned. "Ford was in town two weeks ago?"

"Ford, is it?" Charity grinned. "Two weeks ago almost to the day. He was sitting right over there at that table by the window. I couldn't believe it when I saw him and Betty told me who he was."

Roz couldn't believe her ears. He hadn't mentioned being in Timber Falls before. "You're sure it was Ford Lancaster?"

"Tall, dark and intense?" Charity said.

"That's him. But you left out conceited, rude and generally nasty." Except in the shower. "Charity, he thinks my father's fall wasn't an accident. He thinks someone might have pushed him. We're going up into the mountains this morning to see if we can find any evidence.'' She didn't mention the ''bones'' her father had supposedly found right before his ''accident.''

''We?'' Charity echoed.

''Don't get any ideas. I wouldn't trust Ford as far as I could throw him.'' Ford had left out the part about him being here two weeks ago. Before her father had gone into the woods? Or right after?

''It seems odd he would be worried about your father.''

''Doesn't it though. It turns out that Ford is the son of John Wells, Dad's good friend who used to hike with him? Ford's parents divorced when he was young and his mother remarried, thus the Lancaster.''

''Aha,'' Charity said. ''So he wrote that article about your father's photos—and *his* father. Oooo, small world, huh?''

Roz nodded. ''Tell me about it. Not only that, strange things have been happening ever since I hit town. Even before I arrived.'' She told Charity about what she'd seen at Lost Creek Falls.

''Roz, that's horrible.''

''And last night...'' She sighed. ''I walked in my sleep.'' She didn't want to get into all the details, especially the part about Ford Lancaster saving her— again—if he was to be believed. Or about the possibility that she'd been drugged—if she actually had been.

''I'm not sure of anything or anyone at this point,'' Roz admitted. ''Especially Ford Lancaster. He seems to always turn up whenever I need him.''

Charity quirked a brow. "Not a bad thing to have in a man."

Roz had to laugh. "You are such a romantic. Ford Lancaster is the most arrogant, infuriating, obstinate man I've ever met."

"So you say," Charity said with a half smile.

Wishing she hadn't let the friendship lapse, Roz reached across the table for Charity's hand. "It really is good to see you. I missed you so much, but after my mother...died, I just couldn't face Timber Falls."

"I know. I should have made an effort to get up to Seattle more often," Charity said. "Just tell me what I can do to help your dad."

"There is nothing at this point except mention him in your prayers."

"You got it. So you and Ford are looking for some sort of evidence that it wasn't an accident."

Ford had warned Roz not to mention to anyone that her father might have found something in the woods that might be Bigfoot bones. If word got out, everyone and his brother would be up there looking, trying to solve the mystery and making it even harder for her and Ford. There were enough people in town looking for Bigfoot as it was.

"We just want to take a look," Roz said. "I'm not convinced but it gives me something positive to do while I'm waiting for Dad to regain consciousness. I'm sure once he does, he'll be able to tell us what happened."

Charity nodded. "Hopefully, he just fell and that's all there is to it. I'd hate to think anyone would hurt Liam."

"Me, too." Roz had left her cell phone number with the hospital. Now she gave the number to Charity.

Betty slid the breakfast special in front of Roz, and refilled her coffee cup and Charity's diet cola. The café was filling up fast so Betty only visited for a minute and was gone.

"It must be hard for you to come back here, especially to stay in the house," Charity said.

Roz nodded, tears stinging her eyes. "I miss Mom so much. Being in that house just makes me wonder why she did it, you know?"

"Yeah. That is one of the hardest things about a suicide when there is no note. You always wonder why."

Roz wiped her tears and looked toward the street as a bright red sports car swung into a parking space out front and a young dark-haired woman emerged. She stalked toward the café, flinging open the door, and charged toward their booth, the bell tinkling wildly behind her.

Roz watched in shock as the woman stormed over to them, gaze locked on Charity, a newspaper rolled up in her hand.

"Stop printing lies about my father!" the woman screamed, throwing the rolled-up paper at Charity. "I've warned you. If you say another word about my father I'll…I'll burn that stupid newspaper of yours to the ground with you in it!"

The woman turned and stormed back out. Roz watched in amazement as the brunette climbed into the red sports car and sped off, tires squealing. "Who was that?"

Charity was busy ironing the wrinkles out of the newspaper on the café table—and smiling. "You didn't recognize her? No, I guess you wouldn't since she went to private school and was seldom home during her formative years. That was Wade Dennison's daughter, Desiree."

Roz stared at her friend. "Dennison Ducks?" She looked after the red sports car, then down at the headline in today's paper.

Turning the newspaper so she could read the first part of the story, Roz learned that Wade Dennison's gun had been used to kill his foreman Bud Farnsworth, and that Farnsworth had allegedly been involved in the kidnapping of Angela Dennison and responsible for the murder of Nina Monroe, one of the decoy painters at the plant.

"Charity? You were almost killed?"

She nodded, then said conspiratorially, "There are some people in this town who believe Wade shut Bud up before he could implicate him in the kidnapping."

Roz was shaking her head in disbelief. "You think Wade was involved in his own daughter's kidnapping?"

"I said 'some' people."

"Right." Roz wished she didn't know her friend so well. "Charity, Desiree just threatened to burn down your newspaper with you in it. I think you should call Mitch and tell him."

Charity's eyes twinkled. "Maybe you're right

about calling Mitch.'' She smiled and toyed with the bracelet on her wrist.

''A gift from Mitch?'' Roz asked, admiring the bracelet.

Charity nodded shyly.

Roz felt a stab of envy. Charity had never wavered when it came to her love for Mitch. Roz had never known any man who could make *her* look like that, and her fear was that she never would. Hearing the café door open again, she turned and realized she was hoping to see Ford Lancaster fill that doorway.

MITCH SPOTTED the dark blue pickup parked in the lot at Lost Creek Falls as he pulled in. He parked his cruiser and walked to the top of the falls in time to see Ford Lancaster clambering up the steep side of the creek gorge.

Lancaster didn't seem in the least surprised to see him. But he did look guilty—something Mitch had come to recognize after ten years as a sheriff in a remote part of Oregon.

''Morning, Sheriff,'' Lancaster said casually enough. He was younger than Mitch had expected, and reminded Mitch a little of his older brother Jesse. There was a wildness about him that Ford Lancaster seemed to keep well hidden behind his no-nonsense scientist veneer.

What worried Mitch was that Ford seemed to have already conned Roz. And now Ford Lancaster was at the site of an alleged suicide. What was he doing here? More to the point, what was he doing back in Timber Falls? And just how involved was he with

Roz—and Liam Sawyer? Enough that he thought Liam needed protection. Now why was that?

They were all answers Mitch planned to get. "Looking for something?"

"Same thing you are." Ford's pale aquamarine eyes gave nothing away.

Mitch would have distrusted him just based on what he knew of him. He definitely didn't like him hanging around Roz.

"Did you find the body?" Mitch asked. Which begged the question, why Ford Lancaster would risk his neck to climb down into the gorge to look for a body to begin with when he'd already said he didn't see anyone jump and thought Rozalyn Sawyer had just imagined it.

"There is no body."

"Is that right?" Mitch marveled at the man's arrogance. "What makes you so sure of that?" Bodies often got caught in the rocks or in tree limbs and didn't come up for weeks, even months.

"I found this." Ford stuck his hand in his pocket. Mitch was startled to see what he withdrew. A mannequin's hand, the painted bright red nails chipped.

"There are broken parts all down the creek about a quarter mile."

Mitch took the piece of plastic and turned it in his fingers. "You think this is what Roz saw last night? A mannequin falling off the top of the falls?" He frowned down at the slightly curved fingers.

"Someone hid in the trees at the top of the falls and pushed it off, yes, that's exactly what I think."

Mitch glanced toward the large old pine that grew out over the rocks at the top of the waterfall. "It was pouring last night. Odd time for a prank."

Ford nodded as Mitch shifted his gaze back to him. "There was a detour sign in the middle of the highway at the falls turnoff. Whoever planned this knew about what time Rozalyn would be coming up that road."

"Someone staged this explicitly for her?" Mitch asked in surprise. "Why?"

Ford shook his head. "All I know is that I found some footprints where I think he waited for her to drive up. He already had the mannequin hidden in the trees at the top of the falls. When she started to turn around, he rushed through her headlights wearing a bright yellow raincoat so she couldn't miss him."

"Roz said she thought the jumper was a *woman*," Mitch pointed out.

Ford nodded. "If you ask Rozalyn, I'm willing to bet she'd tell you the person had the hood up on the raincoat the first time she saw him or her. Anyway, as I was saying, the person rushed to the top of the falls, made the switch behind that tree, putting the raincoat on the mannequin and pushed it off, staying hidden in the trees and darkness. I think he or she stayed hidden long enough to witness Rozalyn's reaction—or lay in wait."

Mitch shook his head. "Don't tell me. He planned to push Roz off the falls." This man seemed to have all the answers.

Ford shrugged. "I don't think the person who did this expected me to be on the road last night—let alone that I would race back to save her. I was starting to drive off. If I hadn't glanced in my side mirror and seen her go tearing over to the falls, who knows what would have happened.''

"That makes you a hero," Mitch said. Not likely.

Ford made a face as if he couldn't see himself a hero any more than Mitch could. "It's just my theory of what happened.''

Mitch nodded. "And a damned interesting one, too. You seem to have it all worked out. Lucky for Roz that you were here." Or was it?

FORD COULD HEAR the accusation in the sheriff's tone. He'd known what he was up against. He was an outsider in this close-knit community. Worse, his name seemed to be legend.

"As a scientist, I've uncovered my share of hoaxes," he said.

"Yes, I recall that about you. Handy that when we find your prints on this hand you have an explanation for that, too.''

Ford gritted his teeth, curbing his impatience. "You have a better theory than mine'.''

"Not yet. Where was this person's vehicle?"

"I would imagine it was hidden in the trees. I found an old logging road up that way.'' He pointed to the south. "It's practically grown in. The driver would have had to know it was there."

"Someone local then?"

Ford shrugged. "Or someone who had a map of the old logging roads around here." That definitely opened up the possibilities.

"How many people knew what time Roz was supposed to arrive?"

"I wouldn't know, Sheriff." But he knew someone had laid in wait for Rozalyn Sawyer up here last night. He didn't have an ounce of solid proof. The mannequin, the footprints, all circumstantial. But he knew in his heart that this whole show had been for her.

What he didn't know was why. Or if it had only been to scare her—or kill her. He'd know that when he got the results from the urinalysis. If the chocolate she ingested last night was drugged…

"You've certainly taken an interest in Roz's well-being as well as her father's."

Ford smiled. "Don't beat around the bush, Sheriff. You want to know why I just happen to be there every time Rozalyn needs me?" He shrugged. "I wish I knew. Just lucky, I guess."

"Let's try a question you can answer. What are you doing in Timber Falls?"

Ford hesitated. He wished now that he'd let the sheriff find the mannequin downstream on his own and come up with his own conclusions as well. "Isn't it possible I just came to town to investigate the Bigfoot sightings and got caught up in the Sawyers' lives?"

"No," Mitch said. "You're holding out on me, Lancaster. I'm thinking I should run you in for further questioning."

Ford looked toward the falls. He needed his freedom, whatever price it took. "You'll hear about this sooner or later anyway. Liam's best friend was my father.''

"John Wells?'' Mitch asked, in obvious surprise.

Ford explained how his parents had divorced when he was young, how his mother had remarried, his stepfather had adopted him and he hadn't seen much of his biological father—until two days ago when he'd been with him when he died.

"I guess that explains the article you did on Liam,'' the sheriff said.

"I guess.''

"Great job you have, making fools of people in print.''

"It pays the bills,'' Ford said with a shrug.

The sheriff didn't even try to hide his contempt. "It still doesn't answer my question.''

"My father just passed away. Before he did, I promised him I'd try to make amends with Liam for what I did.'' Lying was becoming almost too easy.

The sheriff studied him for a long moment, then nodded. "I'll keep this if you don't mind,'' he said, pocketing the mannequin hand.

As if Ford had a choice. "There's more of the body downstream about a half mile.'' He hesitated, then jumped in with both feet. "Do me a favor. Take a look at Rozalyn's mother's suicide.''

The sheriff frowned. "Why?''

Ford shook his head. "Just a feeling.''

"You have a lot of those, don't you?'' His gaze seemed to soften. "This is about Rozalyn, isn't it?''

Ford looked toward the falls again but said nothing. He hated being so transparent. He wanted to give

Rozalyn some peace of mind. Had Anna Sawyer gone up those stairs, climbed out on that widow's walk and taken a dive all on her own? Worse, was it possible Rozalyn might have done the same thing last night—if he hadn't stopped her? He wished the lab would call back. He found himself praying there were drugs in that chocolate. He didn't want to even think about the alternative.

"I'm just curious about the case, all right?" he said at last, kicking himself mentally for getting involved with the woman. But involved he was. And in ways he didn't even want to think about.

"What specifically am I looking for?" Mitch asked.

"Inconsistencies. You remember the case?"

Mitch nodded. "I was undersheriff then, getting ready to take over for our sheriff who was retiring. But all of that information is confidential."

Ford nodded, knowing the sheriff would pull out the old file and, if there was something there, would use it to help Rozalyn. Mission accomplished.

Without another word, Ford turned and started toward his pickup wondering if the sheriff was really going to let him walk that easily. He had a piece of the mannequin's face in his pocket that he'd saved to show Rozalyn and that he didn't want the sheriff to know about.

"You're not planning to leave town for a while, are you?" the sheriff called after him.

Ford wanted nothing more than to get in his pickup and drive away from all of this—especially the lies. But as he opened his truck door, he looked back at the sheriff and the falls. It was too easy to imagine someone hiding in that warped old pine at the top. He couldn't leave now. He was in too deep.

"Don't worry, Sheriff. I'll be here."

Chapter Ten

Mitch hadn't thought about the Anna Sawyer case in years. Sheriff Tim "Hud" Hudson had done all the real investigating on the case but he'd talked to Mitch about it. Several things had been troubling about it.

Anna hadn't left a note, which wasn't all that rare in a suicide. What had bothered Hud was a visit by the interim local doctor just minutes before Anna had committed suicide. Liam had passed a car driving going too fast on the road out, and had been forced to drive into the shallow ditch to miss it.

Liam hadn't been able to see the person driving because of the sun glare on the windshield but he'd recognized the car. It was Dr. Morrow's car, Anna's physician.

Hud's first thought was that the doc had come out to give Anna bad news, but that theory hadn't panned out. According to Anna's medical records, she'd been fine.

Liam had tried unsuccessfully to reach Dr. Morrow later only to discover the man had left town. Left two weeks earlier than he'd planned. Hud didn't have any luck reaching the doc, either. He was told by the doctor's nurse that Dr. Morrow had decided to take a trip and couldn't be reached. Then Hud had retired and Mitch had taken over and that part of the investigation had fallen through the cracks.

Another thing that had troubled Hud was the fact that Rozalyn had been in the house the day her mother committed suicide. The then-teenager had been in her room with her stereo on. But later she recalled hearing voices in the attic and something heavy hitting the floor.

When Hud reached the house though, he found no sign that anyone else had been there other than the doctor—nor any sign of a struggle.

Hud had wondered if there'd been something going on between Anna Sawyer and the doc since Dr. Morrow closed up his practice and left town so suddenly. A love affair gone wrong? Hud hadn't bought that since he'd known Anna and believed her happy in her marriage. But without talking to the doctor to see what he'd been doing there that day…

Now ten years had passed. Even if there was something in the old file, it wouldn't bring Anna Sawyer back. Nor would it necessarily give Roz any peace.

But Mitch knew he was going to have to take a look anyway.

Roz was only momentarily disappointed when the person coming in through the door at Betty's Café wasn't Ford Lancaster. She'd hoped he'd finished his errands early and had come to pick her up.

Instead it was Charity's aunt Florie who came in a gust of wind.

"Brace yourself," Charity said.

Florie was dressed just as Roz remembered: a flowing colorful caftan, dyed bright red hair wound turban-style around her small head, and blue eyes glittering beneath a smear of turquoise eye shadow. It felt so good to see that some things never changed.

Roz slid from the booth to hug the elderly woman.

"I couldn't believe it when I looked into my coffee grounds and saw that you were coming back to town," Florie said, holding her at arm's length studying her a moment before sliding into the booth across from Roz, next to her niece. "Are you all right? I was worried about you. I'm sorry your homecoming hasn't been a happy one."

"Thank you," Roz said, sitting back down across from them.

Betty called to Florie across the room. "Just coffee," Florie called back and turned to Charity. "I have some news for you."

Charity looked skeptical. "Tell me this news didn't come via the stars."

Florie made a face at her. "One of these days you're going to take my sight seriously. One of these days soon," she said ominously, "you'll be begging me for a reading."

"Uh-huh," Charity said. "What news?"

"Daisy Dennison," Florie said as if announcing the topic.

Clearly, she had her niece's full attention now. "The last time I saw Daisy she was in a hospital in Eugene recovering from a gunshot wound," Charity said.

Florie nodded.. "Well she's home and *cleaning* house." Roz could almost hear the drumroll. "Daisy threw Wade out."

Charity lifted a brow. "That house is his pride and joy. He'd never leave it."

"He's living in one of my units," Florie said. "Moved in late last night and let me tell you his aura looked bad."

"I don't believe it," Charity said. "For him to move out of the house—" She looked from her aunt to Roz. "Do you know what this means?"

Roz shook her head. "Not a clue."

"Daisy *knows* he was in on the kidnapping. And he knows she knows. She's got him over a barrel and is calling the shots now."

"Why doesn't she tell Mitch?" Roz asked, noticing the clouds outside.

"Probably for the same reason Mitch hasn't arrested Wade," Charity said, clearly excited about this news. "A distinct lack of evidence. The evidence seems to have died with Bud Farnsworth. We may never know what happened to Angela Dennison now."

"How horrible," Roz said. As kids, they'd believed that Angela was buried in the woods behind the Dennison house. Once on Halloween, when they'd gone to the Dennison house to trick-or-treat, Charity swore she heard a baby crying and turned to see what she believed to be Angela's ghost behind her.

"Wade must have found out that the baby wasn't his and got rid of it," Charity whispered. "A man with an ego like his, he probably couldn't live with the thought that he might be raising another man's child."

"Worse, falling in love with that child," Roz said.

"You're right," Charity said. "That must be why he had Angela kidnapped so quickly after she was born. He couldn't risk bonding with the baby only to find out it was another man's—and a constant reminder of his wife's infidelity."

"I think there are few men who could handle that kind of knowledge," Roz said. "But what if he was wrong? What if he got rid of his *own* daughter?"

Charity shook her head, obviously unable to imagine. "Unless that baby's body turns up, we will never know who the father really was. Maybe Daisy doesn't even know herself."

Florie hadn't said anything for several minutes but Roz saw her shiver as she reached for her coffee cup and knocked it over. "Clumsy," Florie muttered under her breath as coffee spilled across the table.

"What's wrong?" Roz asked, seeing Florie's expression.

Florie was shaking her head, staring at the spilled coffee as if it were spilled blood. "Liam. Have you heard from him since he went into the woods after the most recent Bigfoot sighting?"

Roz and Charity exchanged a surprised look.

"Auntie, I thought you knew," Charity said. "Liam was found last night."

"Something happened to him! I knew it." All the color drained from Florie's face. She grabbed the edge of the table. "I saw his misery in the cards but

I thought it was his marriage…." She looked up at Roz.

"He's in the hospital. Mitch thinks he fell from a cliff. He's in a coma," Roz told her.

Tears welled in Florie's wizened eyes.

Charity put an arm around her aunt's shoulder as Roz reached across the table to take one of the woman's bejeweled hands.

"I thought you had heard," Charity said.

"I was on the Internet working most of the night and morning," Florie whispered. Roz knew that Florie had her own Web site and did psychic readings via e-mail.

"Are you all right?" Roz asked, surprised the woman was so upset.

"I have to go splash my face with cold water." She rose unsteadily.

"I'll go with you," Roz said.

Florie waved her off. "I'll be fine. I just need a moment alone."

"Should we let her go by herself?" Roz asked in concern as Florie traipsed off to the ladies' room.

"She'll be fine. She hates being fussed over. She's been in a tizzy ever since Liam remarried—and she wasn't the bride," Charity said. "Ah, unrequited love."

Roz blinked. "Your aunt is in love with my father?" she asked in disbelief.

"Has been for years. I thought you knew. She says she saw it in the stars. She and your father. Every time Liam came up to check the house or make repairs, Florie just happened to stop by with some fresh-baked goods for him. Tofu or carob chips. No wonder he married someone else.''

''Emily can't boil water,'' Roz said, still shocked by the news about Florie and Liam. Did Liam have any idea of her feelings? Men could be so dense sometimes.

''Florie's coming back,'' Charity whispered. ''Don't mention Emily. You'll just get her started. She thinks Emily is only after your father's money and somehow tricked him into marrying her.''

''That's exactly what I think,'' Roz said.

''Florie's never even seen the woman—except in her coffee grounds,'' Charity confided.

Florie returned, full of questions about Liam. Roz did her best to answer them.

''Uh-oh,'' Charity said under her breath as she looked out the café window.

Roz followed her gaze. Emily was coming up the street, her blond head peering out from under a dark umbrella. Roz looked over at Florie as Emily swept past the window.

''Don't do it, Aunt Florie,'' Charity said.

''Do what?'' the older woman asked innocently as she crossed herself even though she wasn't Catholic.

''Just don't.'' Charity shook her head at Roz. ''Don't believe anything she tells you.''

''All I'm going to say is that someone should warn the woman,'' Florie said. ''Emily is about to come to a bad end.''

''It's just jealousy talking,'' Charity said.

''I'm not jealous,'' Florie argued. ''Liam deserves better, that's for sure, but my feelings toward his…wife have nothing to do with what I see for her future. She isn't long for this world.''

"Only if she meets you in a dark alley," Charity said, obviously trying to laugh off her aunt's prediction.

"She doesn't believe I have the sight," Florie said, unperturbed to Roz.

"She did when we were *kids*," Roz said.

Charity groaned. "We were kids. It was fun. Now, it's…different."

Emily came out of the drug store next door and stopped just feet from them at the curb. As she closed her umbrella and reached for the door handle of Drew's sports car as he pulled up for her, Florie let out a gasp.

"I've seen that woman somewhere before, a long time ago," Florie said.

Charity rolled her eyes so only Roz could see.

"Except her hair used to be a different color," Florie was saying. "It's been years but I never forget an aura and that woman's is dark as sin."

"Auntie, you're either confusing her with someone else or—"

"I know where I saw her," Florie said, eyes wide. "It was here in Timber Falls only…only it was years ago."

Charity looked even more skeptical. "She's from Portland and I'm positive I heard she'd never been to Timber Falls before Liam brought her here after the wedding." She looked at Roz for confirmation.

Roz nodded. "This is the first time you've seen her since she married Dad and moved here?"

"She's kept to herself since she hit town," Charity said. "Few people have seen her except in passing."

Emily didn't fit in here and must have realized it. "She was married to some hotshot lawyer in Portland and part of the social whirl, I guess," Roz said. "He died about a year ago and left her well off."

Florie let out a "humph." "If that were true, she wouldn't have had to snag Liam six months later."

Charity did another eye roll, but Roz thought Florie had a good point. Was it possible Emily had exaggerated about her rich, famous lawyer husband? Or even outright lied? Liam wouldn't have checked up on Emily. He took everyone at his or her word. But Roz had no problem with doing some checking. And she could see that Charity was thinking the same thing.

"It's how she's dressed that's throwing me off," Florie mumbled. "She was wearing something… different." Her face lit up. "A uniform! A nurse's uniform. That's it! She worked for that young doctor who filled in for a while when Doc Purdy broke his leg. Morrow that was his name. James Morrow. A real looker he was, and married."

Charity was staring at her aunt. "I remember that woman. She was brunette and much chubbier."

Florie nodded enthusiastically. "You think that blond doesn't come out of a bottle? *Please.* And she was heavier because I think she was pregnant with the young doctor's baby."

"Are you sure you didn't see this on some soap opera?" Charity teased. "Auntie, you have Emily Sawyer mixed up with some other woman."

Florie was shaking her head. "I can almost remember her name."

"Don't look at me. Hope, Faith and I went into Eugene to that woman doctor down there," Charity said of her and her sisters.

"I remember Doc Purdy breaking his leg," Roz said. "But Dr. Morrow..."

"You should remember him," Florie said. "Didn't your mother see him professionally during the time right before—" She broke off realizing what she was about to say. Right before Anna Sawyer killed herself.

"Dr. Morrow," Roz said slowly.

"Roz, you must have seen her," Florie said, not letting it drop.

She shook her head. "The doctor came to the house alone or Mom went to his office." But why had her mother been going to the doctor? She remembered her dad trying to find out, but couldn't remember what he'd found out other than her mother hadn't been diagnosed with cancer or anything that would make her want to commit suicide.

Dr. Morrow hadn't stayed long after her mother's death, the memory coming back now. She could recall little about him except that he was nice. And he had made at least one house call, the day her mother died. She couldn't remember any scandal involving the man's nurse but then she didn't remember ever seeing her.

Roz looked up to see that Charity and Florie were looking at her with sympathy in their eyes.

Charity took a bite of her pie, then pushed the plate

away. "Did I tell you about that guy we used to go to school with, Arnie—"

"Lynette. That was her name," Florie exclaimed. "I knew it would come to me. Lynette…"

"You see where I get it," Charity joked and tried again to change the subject. "I was raised on gossip. What other career path could I have taken but journalism?"

"Why can't I think of her last name?" Florie muttered to herself. "Charity, wasn't she the woman who took care of you when you sprained your ankle wrestling with that boy that time at the hospital?"

"It wasn't just some boy. It was Mitch," Charity said and grinned. "And Kate Clark was the emergency room nurse. Dr. Morrow was already gone by then and his nurse, as well."

"Kate's taking care of Dad," Roz said. "And a doctor named…Harris?"

"Mark Harris," Charity said nodding. "He took the job here about a month ago. It's so hard to get doctors to stay in Timber Falls. Too isolated and the money's not that great."

"Hargrove," Florie said and snapped her fingers. "Her name was Lynette Hargrove."

Charity shook her head. "Auntie, it's not the same woman, okay? Give it a rest."

Florie wasn't paying attention. She had reached into her purse and now took out a small velvet bag. From the bag she withdrew a set of worn tarot cards.

"Auntie, don't do this, okay?"

Florie didn't pay her niece any mind.

Betty came over to refill the coffee cups and Charity's diet cola. She stood for a moment and watched Florie adeptly deal out three cards, then close her eyes tightly before placing a card facedown on top of each of them.

One of the patrons called to Betty. It was obvious she hated to leave but had to.

Roz watched, mesmerized as Florie slowly turned over the first card and then pressed her hand to her mouth, tears swimming in her eyes. "Liam is going to regain consciousness," she whispered and smiled over at Roz.

Charity said nothing as Florie turned over the next card and frowned. Her gaze came up to meet Roz. "But he will only be in more danger." She turned over the third card and let out a gasp as her gaze flew up to Roz.

"What is it?" Roz cried.

Florie had gone deathly pale again. With shaking hands she hurriedly scooped up the cards. "It's nothing." She dropped the pack of cards back into the velvet bag and thrust them deep into her purse.

"See why I hate it when she does this?" Charity said to Roz. "You scare people, Auntie."

But Roz could see that Florie had scared herself, as well. Tears welled in the older woman's eyes and she was still visibly shaking.

"Florie, you have to tell me what you saw," Roz pleaded clutching at the woman's arm. "I know Dad is in danger. I need to know what you saw. Please."

Florie's voice broke as she whispered, "I saw an open dirt grave with…the *bones* still in it."

Roz felt all the air rush from her. *"Bones?"*

"*Old* bones." The woman shuddered and stumbled to her feet. "I have to go to the hospital and see Liam." Without another word, she hurried off, her brightly colored caftan blowing in the breeze behind her, leaving Roz to stare after her in shock and growing fear.

Charity gave Roz a ride back to the house since it was raining again, a light drizzle that made the once sunny day as dreary and dark as her mood. Roz avoided the main house, walking around to the guest house through the garden.

The chill she suddenly felt had nothing to do with the light rain. Someone was watching her. She stopped to look toward the main house but, in the dull light, couldn't see if anyone was looking out of the attic windows.

She felt spooked and afraid and couldn't wait to see Ford. She had never thought she'd admit it, but she was glad he was here. Glad they would be looking for the bones together.

Florie's revelations still had her reeling. Bones. And her conviction that Emily wasn't really Emily Lane but some woman named Lynette Hargrove, a former nurse in Timber Falls. A nurse who'd worked for the doctor who'd been taking care of Roz's mother.

Florie had to be wrong. Liam would have mentioned if Emily had ever been a nurse. Especially in Timber Falls. Unless he hadn't known. And what about the name change? Lynette Hargrove. It couldn't be the same woman.

Roz was disappointed to find Ford hadn't returned.

She checked her watch. He was late. Because he was a scientist, she'd somehow expected him to be more exacting than this. Maybe he'd been held up.

A sliver of worry began to fester inside her at the thought that something might have happened to him. If he'd gone off asking questions about Liam…

She stepped up onto the porch out of the rain and tried the door. He'd left it unlocked for her. That was considerate.

As she stepped in, she heard something and realized she wasn't alone. The rustle of papers came from the bedroom. She didn't close the door, instead stepped into the guest house quietly to peer around the corner into the bedroom.

He had his back to her and appeared to be going through something on a desk by the bed.

"Drew?"

He swung around, obviously surprised to see her. "I didn't hear you come in."

No, she'd gathered that by his surprise. She looked to the papers in his hands. "What are you doing?"

"I had to see what Ford Lancaster was up to." He put the papers back on the desk and moved toward her. "I'm worried about you. I can see that you're starting to trust him."

Right now she trusted Ford more than she did Drew, she realized. She took a step back, glad she'd left the door open.

Drew stopped advancing toward her, looking hurt. "I'm sorry if I scared you. Roz, I was upstairs earlier looking for you and I noticed the door open to your mom's old sewing room and the broken record on the floor.''

She held her breath.

''You're going to think I'm crazy but a few weeks ago I heard that record playing,'' he said. ''I went up and turned off the phonograph but it came right back on. Blew me away. I unplugged it but the next night I heard it again. Totally freaked me out.''

She found herself nodding. ''It did that last night.''

He laughed. ''I was afraid of that.'' The smile died on his lips. ''I *am* worried about you.''

''I appreciate that,'' she said, feeling a little more at ease with him. ''Drew, phonographs don't plug themselves back in.''

''I know. I caught my mother in that room several nights later.''

His admission surprised her.

''I know she's jealous of you,'' he said. ''She resents the fact that Liam insisted on returning to Timber Falls because of you.''

''Because of *me?* But I live in Seattle.''

Drew nodded. ''Your dad has this idea that one day you will come back here with your own family and settle in Timber Falls in the house where you were raised.''

Roz couldn't believe her ears. Her father had never said anything to her about it.

''He keeps talking about your kids racing through the old house, putting laughter back in it and how Anna would have wanted that desperately. You can imagine how that makes my mother feel.''

"So you think she rigged the phonograph to... scare me away?"

"I think it's possible. If you don't come back to Timber Falls, then your father will eventually move her somewhere so they can have a fresh start. She really hates it here."

Roz could see how hard the admission was for him. He was protective of his mother. But he was obviously worried about Roz and maybe what lengths his mother might go to.

"Do you know who left me the chocolates by my bed last night?"

Drew seemed surprised by the question. "I did. Didn't you get my note? They were all right, weren't they?"

She nodded, even though she wasn't sure about that. "You didn't happen to hear me walking in my sleep last night, did you?"

His eyes widened. "No. I hope you avoided the stairs."

"I didn't walk far," she said and looked toward the desk where she'd found Drew going through a stack of papers.

"You're wrong to trust Ford," Drew said, following her gaze. "Roz, look what he did to your father. I wish my mother had never told him he could stay in the guest house. I'll tell her to kick him out."

"No," Roz said.

He looked at her with obvious concern. "You don't really think he's in town to help your dad, do you? Men like him don't change."

Her greatest fear. It was obvious from Drew's expression that he could see that he'd struck a chord.

"He wants something, Roz, and you have to ask yourself what," Drew continued. "He acts as if he's protecting Liam, but what if it's just the opposite? What if he doesn't want any of us in the hospital room when Liam wakes up because Ford Lancaster has something to hide?"

Her cell phone rang, startling her.

"Just think about it," Drew said and headed for the door. "In the meantime, be careful."

She wondered if he meant because of Ford. Or his mother. Roz was still chilled by what Florie had seen in the cards. Now she wondered if Emily really might not be the person she was pretending to be.

The phone rang again. Roz checked the number. Charity.

"I didn't want to say anything in front of my aunt but I did some quick checking on Emily," Charity said without preamble.

Roz had known she would. She held her breath.

"There was a hotshot attorney named Andrew Lane who died about a year ago. According to his obit, he is survived by his wife, Emily, and two grown children, Andrew Junior and Suzanne of Portland, Oregon."

Roz let out the breath she'd been holding.

"As for Lynette Hargrove, she died in a car wreck about a year after she left Timber Falls," Charity said. "You see why I warned you not to listen to Aunt Florie? So just ignore that thing about bones, okay?"

She wished she could. "Thank you so much."

"No problem. Better to set your mind at ease."

Roz couldn't agree more as she snapped off her phone. She just wished Charity could ease her mind about Ford. Why wasn't he back yet? She was starting to worry about him.

It was quiet inside the guest house. Roz checked the bathroom, remembering the urine sample she'd left on the back of the bathroom sink. It was gone. He must have taken it to the lab.

Was that the only errand he had to run this morning? She hoped she'd just been sleepwalking, and that there was no plot against her or her father.

She turned and looked toward the desk where she'd caught Drew. Ford's laptop sat on top of what appeared to be a stack of papers that had been hurriedly shoved under it. Drew's doing? Or Ford's?

Stepping toward it, she saw the corner of a magazine article sticking out from the pile of papers. She recognized the photograph. It was one her father had taken of a large hairy creature he and John Wells had seen deep in the Cascades and believed was Bigfoot.

She lifted the laptop and pulled the jumble of papers from beneath it. On the top was the piece Ford Lancaster had written about her father for a scientific journal along with various newspaper articles quoting Lancaster and his experts speculating on how Liam Sawyer had manufactured the fraudulent Bigfoot photographs.

She stared down at the photograph of her father for a moment, then ruffled through the other papers. They were all articles about Bigfoot. One headline caught her attention: One Million Dollar Reward Offered For

Bigfoot Evidence. The article said the man would pay for definitive proof that a Bigfoot existed. At the bottom, how to contact the man to collect had been circled.

Heart in her throat, she sifted through the papers and found what appeared to be the beginning of a new article typed double-space on plain white paper. It was entitled Bigfoot Hysteria In Timber Falls: Home Of The Infamous Photographer by Ford Lancaster.

''Oh God,'' she breathed, tears burning her eyes as she saw her father's name in the first paragraph of the story.

She stumbled back, all the papers slipping from her fingers and fluttering to the floor except for the old article about her father. She balled it up in her hands. She should have listened to that nagging feeling she'd had about Ford. But she'd thought she didn't trust him because he made her feel things she had never felt with any other man. Like hatred, she told herself angrily. Not desire. Dammit, not desire ever again.

She couldn't believe how naive she'd been, she thought as she threw the article about her father across the room. Ford had lied about everything. And she'd just wanted to believe he'd lied about a stupid kiss.

He didn't feel guilty about what he'd done to her father—or to his own. He was only in this for the money. Or the notoriety. Or both.

Hadn't she known deep down inside he wasn't telling her the real reason he was here risking his life? Why he insisted her father be protected? Just to get

closer to her. All he wanted was to find the bones—
or whatever had put her father in danger.

Oh Roz, you fool, you. She thought about how Ford
had been in the shower with her last night, how he'd
kissed her. Not once but twice. Tears sprang to her
eyes. *He was just trying to gain your trust, you silly
goose. He planned to use you to help him. Don't you
remember that look you caught in his eyes at the
café? He thinks he has you right where he wants you.*

He *did,* she thought. But not anymore.

She was so angry her first instinct was to wait for
him to return and confront him. While that might
make her feel better, it wouldn't help her father. No,
she had to find the bones, bones her father had mis-
takenly told Ford about—and she had to do it before
Ford did.

Unlike Ford, her father wouldn't have sold the
bones to the highest bidder. Nor would she.

As Roz left the guest house and got into her car,
she still couldn't shake the feeling that someone was
watching her. Where was Ford? And what did he have
planned next for her? She hated to think as she drove
out to the highway and headed toward Maple Creek
Bridge Road.

She couldn't help glancing in her rearview mirror.
How much of what Ford had told her was a lie? Was
her father really in danger? Was *she?* Or had everything that had happened been Ford's doing?

She thought about the person who'd climbed in her
window and went through her suitcase, leaving the
window open—and the suitcase a mess—so she'd
know he'd been there?

Her heart somersaulted in her chest. Ford hadn't left the chocolates. Drew had. Ford couldn't have known her favorites. And anyway, he'd acted as if he hadn't known that Liam had a daughter. That could have been a lie though, too.

But he could have drugged the chocolates when he climbed in through her window. And he could have pretended to rescue her from the widow's walk. For all she knew, he took her up there.

But why go to so much trouble? Because he needed her to trust him. By making her think she was in danger, she had turned to him. She had played right into his hands.

Oh God, how far would he go to get what he wanted?

As far as was needed, she thought, remembering the kisses. And the reward for the Bigfoot bones.

At least now she knew. The only person she had to fear was Ford Lancaster.

Chapter Eleven

When Ford got to the guest house, he couldn't believe Rozalyn hadn't returned given how late he was. After what he'd found in the creek, he had raced back to town, anxious to see her and make sure she was safe.

But how much trouble could she get into since all she had planned was a trip to the hospital and breakfast with her friend?

He opened the guest house door. Had someone come in again? Hadn't the intruder gotten what he'd broken in for the first time?

"Rozalyn?" Ford called.

No answer.

But *someone* had been here. He'd locked the door when he'd left.

The moment he opened the bedroom door he saw the papers on the floor and stopped dead. He'd forgotten all about them after he'd discovered the computer disk gone. Then after he'd brought Roz to the guest house he couldn't very well retrieve them without making her suspicious. He'd planned to take care of them this morning and, in his haste to find out what had happened last night at the falls, he'd forgotten.

That mistake would cost him, he realized, as he picked up the papers and spotted a balled up magazine article he'd started about Liam Sawyer. He swore. Rozalyn had been here. She had come back and found the papers he'd stuffed under the laptop computer after the break-in.

Wait a minute. He didn't make a copy of this article, did he? But here was the article he'd started...

He shoved it away. Nothing mattered now but finding Rozalyn.

Ford swore again as he straightened. He had to find her and try to explain. *Good luck.* She knew the truth. Knew what he considered his father's legacy to him. In the end, John Ford Wells had left him more than his name. He'd left him the chance to be not only wealthy—but also famous. That was one hell of an inheritance.

But he only got it if he found the Bigfoot bones his father's partner had discovered. Funny the way life was. The only fly in the ointment now was Rozalyn Sawyer.

At least he knew where she'd go. Maple Creek Bridge Road. As crazy as she was she'd try to find out the truth on her own. And as crazy as he was, he'd try to save her again.

He grabbed his backpack, threw what he thought he'd need into it and headed for his pickup. He had to find her and quickly. The fool woman was going to get herself killed.

What about the bones?

Screw the bones. For the time being, Rozalyn mattered more.

That realization made him laugh out loud. The woman had put a spell on him. Like he said, life was funny. How else could he explain falling for Liam Sawyer's daughter?

Obviously his life was cursed.

STILL UPSET with her aunt, Charity stopped by the hospital to find Florie sitting by Liam's bedside. She cringed at the thought of what might happen should Emily drop by to see how her husband was doing. That was a confrontation Charity hoped to avoid. After Charity had talked to Roz, she couldn't get Emily and Lynette Hargrove off her mind so she'd put in a couple more calls and was waiting to hear. Florie had to be wrong. And yet, Charity didn't want to take any chances.

And what was that business about bones? What bothered Charity was her friend's reaction. Roz had turned three shades of white over some old bones in a dirt grave. Odd.

Charity watched her aunt through the hospital room window and decided not to interrupt Florie's visit. She left the flowers she'd brought for Liam with the nurse on duty and headed for the newspaper office in the relentless drizzle, windshield wipers flapping. Emily—or whatever her name was—was on her own if she came by the hospital while Florie was there.

A block away, a large figure in a dark raincoat stepped off the curb directly in front of her car. She hit her brakes as Wade Dennison slammed down his palms on the front of her VW Bug, his glaring eyes huge with malice.

Charity scrambled to lock her door, but Wade—for his age—moved too damned fast. He jerked open her car door, his face flushed with anger.

"You meddling bitch!" he bellowed.

Behind her, Charity fumbled for the cell phone in her purse, keeping her hand hidden from Wade's view as she hit the On button, then speed-dialed Mitch's number.

"Listen, Wade—"

"No, you listen to me." Suddenly all the heat went out of him. He seemed to slump against her car, head down, the rain pattering on his raincoat to the sound of…crying?

The unexpected, heart-wrenching sound chased away her fear. She stared at the broken man, suddenly wondering if she could be wrong about him.

"I would never have hurt Angela. Never. I loved her." He looked up, his face wet from the rain, from his tears. "I don't care if she was my daughter by blood. Don't you get it? I love Daisy. She was Daisy's daughter. That's all that ever mattered."

Charity realized now probably wasn't the time to remind him of his words the night Angela disappeared from her crib. But hey, she was a journalist. "You were overheard telling Daisy that you would put her back on the street and take Desiree from her."

His jaw tightened, eyes hard again, and she hoped she wouldn't regret her words. "Those things were said in anger. Daisy knew I would never…" He seemed to lose focus, his head coming up as if he heard something. Or saw something.

Charity followed his gaze and saw a bright red sports car zip by. His daughter, Desiree.

Wade pushed off the car, stumbling back as he turned and walked away, his gait slow and awkward, the movement of a defeated man.

Charity watched him go, stunned by what she'd just seen and heard. Could she be wrong about Wade? But then how did she explain Bud Farnsworth's final moments? It was clear with his dying breath that Bud had been trying to tell Wade something.

She checked her cell phone. She'd reached Mitch's voice mail. She wondered what kind of message she'd left. Mitch wasn't going to like this any better than the newspaper article. She hoped it wouldn't change his mind about that possible marriage proposal he'd started to offer her this morning at Betty's.

ROZ TURNED from the highway onto Maple Creek Bridge Road and followed the narrow, sheltered road until it ended in a small wide spot.

She was glad to see there were no other vehicles parked at the end of the road. But as she looked around, she wondered where her dad's truck and camper were. How odd that the pickup hadn't turned up. Was it possible someone had stolen it? Or dropped him off? Then where were the pickup and camper? More to the point, where was that person and how come he or she hadn't come forward yet?

She realized it was possible her father had hidden his truck and camper—just as he might have hidden the bones he'd found. It didn't sound like him. Liam wasn't one to hide things, to deceive. And because of that, she doubted he would realize the danger of his discovery until it was too late.

With a start, she wondered if someone had moved the truck, hidden it—after that person had pushed her father from the cliff so no one would be looking for him here?

She got out of her SUV, loaded her backpack and tied on her tent and sleeping bag. She considered leaving her camera behind, but realized if she found any proof she'd need it to verify the find. Like her father, she never went anywhere without her camera. She wondered if he'd gotten his discovery on film and where his camera was now. His backpack wasn't at the hospital. That was odd if he'd fallen or even been pushed off a cliff. He would have had it on.

She put enough energy bars and drinking water into her pack to last her a couple of days. She would stay in the mountains tonight, a place where she felt safer than at the house with all its memories and the strange new family. She wasn't taking any chances that she might end up on that widow's walk again.

And she would be a whole lot safer out in the woods than at the guest house with Ford Lancaster, she thought, remembering the kiss and the emotions it stirred in her. And to think she'd been afraid of lowering her defenses around him. What a joke! He hadn't needed to scale the castle walls—she'd dropped the drawbridge.

She shook her head at the memory, pretty sure she really had lost her mind. Because even knowing what a louse he was, she couldn't help remembering the kisses and the feelings and aching for both. *Fool woman.*

She clipped the can of pepper spray to her belt—not so much for a bear encounter as a human one. If anything Ford Lancaster had told her were true, she would be in danger until the bones were secure.

And she now believed her father had found bones. She could just hear Ford if she told him she started believing it when a psychic saw her father—and bones. Ford would have a field day with that.

But what were the chances that Florie would see bones in the tarot cards?

Roz glanced behind her as she swung her backpack over her shoulder, feeling as if she was being followed. But there was no one in the small clearing and it was impossible to see into the thick growth beyond it. Nor had she heard or seen another vehicle on the highway.

She'd noticed that the vacancy sign was back up at the Ho Hum Motel. The Bigfoot hunters were leaving town, giving up since there hadn't been a sighting for several weeks now. Bigfoot sightings this time of year weren't unusual in this area. The theory was that the snow in the higher elevations pushed the elusive creatures down to the rainy areas like Timber Falls.

The Bigfoot sightings had something else in common: they were all on mountain ranges in rugged isolated country. The country beyond this road was unmapped, unexplored and inaccessible except on foot, and there were hundreds of square miles of it.

On this side of the Oregon Cascades a lot of the country wasn't even accessible on foot because of the dense foliage, steep mountain cliffs and numerous waterfalls, streams, lakes and bogs. It was the perfect place for a creature to live and avoid man.

Roz looked up at the rock rims about halfway up the mountain and shivered. That's the area where her father must have been. Whatever he'd discovered had to be fairly close around there, she would think.

She knew she would have to find the bones before Ford Lancaster—and whoever else knew about them. She had no doubt that either would try to stop her.

The moment she stepped from the small clearing where she'd left her SUV, she disappeared into the dark coniferous forest.

She wasn't surprised so few people had ever seen what they believed to be a Bigfoot-like creature. Another life-form could live just yards off the road and remain unseen especially if, as suspected, the creature was nomadic, rare in numbers and knew to avoid man whenever possible.

As she walked, she couldn't shake the feeling though that she wasn't alone. She looked behind her but saw nothing except a dense wall of trees and underbrush. As far as she could tell, there wasn't another human being for miles.

A short way up the trail, she crossed a moss-covered log spanning a gushing stream. The water roared in her ears, reminding her of Lost Creek Falls and what she'd witnessed last night. She wondered if Mitch had found anything. Or if there had been anything to find.

She walked, concentrating on the narrow game trail through the jungle. At one point, she tripped over one

of the tree roots that grew across the path and almost
fell. Resting her hand against a tree trunk, she tried
to catch her breath. Her chest ached and she felt tears
burn her eyes.

A limb snapped off to her right. She froze, listening. She couldn't see anything in the thick vegetation
nor back down the trail behind her. She started walking again. A little faster. By now Ford would know
she wasn't meeting him at the guest house.

Morning gave way to afternoon as she headed for
the band of rocks, stopping only to take a drink or
catch her breath.

"Where had you been, Dad?" she said out loud as
she looked up through the rain and mist at the steep
rock cliffs over the tops of the trees.

She wondered about his state of mind before the
fall and realized she didn't have a clue as to what her
father might have been thinking. He'd married Emily,
hadn't he? That alone made her wonder if she still
knew her father at all.

CHARITY WAS STILL shaken by her run-in with Wade
Dennison. She parked in front of her newspaper office
and sat in her VW bug for a few minutes, trying to
collect herself. As much as she suspected Wade was
a murderer, she hated seeing him the way he'd been
on the street.

Worse, he'd made her wonder if she could be
wrong about him. Sure, he would deny everything,
especially now when it appeared his house of cards
was coming down. But there'd been a ring of truth in
his words. And Charity knew the power of love. If

Wade really had loved Daisy enough to accept not only her affair but possibly the child from that affair—

The passenger side door of her car jerked open and, in a flurry of rain and wind, Sheriff Mitch Tanner slid into the seat next to her.

Charity tried to still her beating heart, this time from being startled out of her wits on the tail of her run-in with Wade. "Hey," she said with less than her usual enthusiasm.

"Are you all right?" Mitch asked, picking up on it.

She told him about her recent encounter with Wade.

"He sounds like he might be losing it," Mitch said when she'd finished. "That could make him even more dangerous."

"I felt sorry for him," she admitted.

"Just don't let your guard down around him, all right? And try not to find yourself alone with him."

She smiled at Mitch's concern. "No dark alleys?"

"Stay away from Dennison Ducks."

He was asking her to back off from her investigation. It was like asking her not to breathe and he had to know that.

"I'll be careful," she said.

He nodded, not looking happy as he opened his door and got out. No kiss. No "see you later." No "how about a late lunch or a romantic dinner?" Or about that earlier proposal that she move in with him. No nothing.

Charity sighed as he got back into his patrol car

and drove away. She waited but he didn't brake or turn around and come back. She opened her door and rushed across the sidewalk through the rain to the *Timber Falls Courier*. But as she opened her office door, she stopped dead. Wade's estranged wife Daisy was sitting in Charity's office chair, obviously waiting for her. Daisy had today's paper in her hand and she was crying.

ROZALYN WAS TOO EASY to find. And that's what worried him. Anyone could figure out where she'd gone.

Ford parked next to her SUV. He hadn't seen any other vehicles on the highway but it would have been easy to hide one in this dense forest, especially with dozens of old trees partially grown in the logging roads. A car could be just a few feet off the road and completely hidden.

Is that why no one had found Liam Sawyer's truck and camper? Ford wished he thought that was the case. That Liam had hid it, but Ford's intellect told him different. Liam wouldn't know to hide his rig anymore than he would have known to hide himself. He wouldn't have realized how much danger he was in until it was too late.

Father like daughter, Ford thought as he got out of his pickup, slung his pack over his shoulder and started up at the mountain. The Cascade Range formed a wall of mile-high peaks from British Columbia to northern California, running the entire length of Oregon. Sixty million years ago this was seabed. The fossilized remains of ancient fish and tropical plants were entombed beneath these mountains and foothills by layers of accumulated lava and ash.

He looked toward the mountains and the band of cliffs that could be seen over the treetops. Walls of columnar basalt, granitic intrusions, ash beds, building-size chunks of andesitic magma that cooled into granite rock.

A scientist's heaven. Or hell, Ford thought as he zipped up his raincoat and pulled up the hood, the drizzle falling around him.

For months Pacific Ocean storms moved inland across the lower Coast Range mountains to the five-thousand-foot wall of the Cascade Mountains, clouds banking up and turning to rain—two hundred inches of the stuff falling each year.

It was the rain that created the long growing season and the lush, jungle-like groves of deciduous and conifer trees, six-hundred-year-old towering Douglas fir, cedar, Western hemlock, vine maple, huckleberry bushes and understories of wild rhododendron tangles, more than thirty types of ferns, four hundred varieties of wildflowers, two hundred species of mushrooms, nine hundred types of thick mosses and twelve hundred species of lichens.

It was a jungle of sorts and the last place on earth he wanted to be. But he had no choice. Rozalyn was up there somewhere and he feared she wasn't alone—and didn't know it.

He followed the narrow animal trail and her tracks through the dense forest, brushing aside the gauzelike yellow drape of Old Man's Beard that hung from tree limbs. The lichen grew up to thirty feet long and several inches thick up here.

Ahead, he caught another glimpse of the band of rock cliffs that ran along the mountainside, and knew that was where Rozalyn would be headed.

It was easy to understand what Liam had been doing up there. The majority of Bigfoot sightings were in places just like it. There were numerous accounts of huge, hairy creatures overturning massive boulders looking for food, stacking the overturned rocks into huge cairns. Another tale told of the creatures throwing the rocks down mountainsides to chase away humans.

He sincerely doubted Rozalyn had to worry about Bigfoot. But who knew what else was in the woods today?

Something else worried him. How the Bigfoot hunters had gotten Liam down. That was a long way to bring him out. True, it was the only way out. A helicopter couldn't land near there. But still, it seemed improbable that some hunters had carried the injured man out because of the liability alone. Maybe that was why they hadn't left their names.

Ford quickened his step, his anxiety growing stronger as he caught glimpses of the cliffs shrouded in cold fog and drizzle. A stream trickled over stair steps of mossy granite. In these two hundred thousand acres of heavily wooded wilderness there were more lakes, ponds, marshes and sloughs than a man could count.

He hated it all. The rain. The dark, dank rainforest of the Cascades. The memory it always brought back from his childhood. It was one of the few places he remembered his father bringing him. It had been shortly after the divorce. Before his father had completely disappeared from their lives.

The memory still made his heart pound with the fear of the nine-year-old boy he'd been. His memory of his father and the Cascades was one of fear. And a knowledge of something he hadn't wanted to know.

Mist moved across the face of the cliffs. He concentrated on finding Roz. Then he'd look for the bones. Bones decomposed quickly in a rainforest. Those that didn't became buried beneath the dense vegetation. If there was a Bigfoot, the theory was that he hid in a cave when he became sick and was about to die. It explained the lack of discovered bones. Because this country was full of caves.

Roz's tracks were easy to follow. Nor could she be far ahead of him. He lengthened his stride, anxious to catch up with her, his discovery at Lost Creek Falls this morning making him more nervous with each step.

Not long after he crossed a huge fallen cedar that spanned a roaring creek, the trail opened into a cool green glen surrounded by the vast forest.

The rain stopped as suddenly as it had begun. He pushed back his hood and stood in the glen, listening for Rozalyn. She couldn't have had that much of a head start on him and still he'd yet to catch her.

He glanced down at the muddy trail. Her footprints held only a little rain. If he kept moving he should catch her by the time she reached the nearest end of the band of rock cliffs.

His cell phone vibrated against his hip, startling him. It surprised him he could get service here. Startled him even more since he'd given the number to only one person.

He hurriedly answered it. "Hello?"

"Mr. Lancaster, I have the results of that urine sample you asked me to put a rush on," the lab tech said.

IT HAD TAKEN Roz longer than she'd expected to reach the bottom of the band of rocks that ran across the mountain—and the old tree where she had often camped with her father.

The rain had stopped momentarily. She took a breather under the tree, adjusted her backpack and stretched. Her body ached. In her career, she did a lot of hiking while carrying all of her camera equipment so she was in pretty good shape.

But today she was trying to hurry. She was winded and tired and discouraged. What did she hope to find up here? If her father really had been pushed, the killer wouldn't have left any evidence. And as for the bones her father had supposedly found, they could be anywhere. Especially if he'd had time to hide them.

She glanced up at the cloud-shrouded band of granite just above her. A hawk circled overhead and close by she could hear a blue jay's call. Up here, she understood why her father loved the Cascades so. There are so few places man can be completely alone, he used to say. And few places that still held mysteries.

Oregon had once been a land of giant bison, mammoth, mastodon, wild horses, giant bear and ground sloth. Today the largest animals were elk. Unless, of course, Bigfoot was an animal—and not a form of human. There was no doubt in her mind there was another lifeform out there—and it was a humanoid.

She had loved to sit around the campfire and listen to her father's stories. He often talked in awe about the day he'd photographed the creature in these woods.

"It had a horrid smell to it," he'd said. "But what got to me was the look in her eyes. It was a female, I'm sure of that. She looked scared, but it was the pleading I saw there, as if she was saying, 'Please, just leave me alone.' I wish I'd never let anyone see those photographs."

Roz thought about that now. If her father had found Bigfoot bones, would he tell anyone? Once there was proof that Bigfoot existed the next step was capturing a live one. Her father would want to prove his earlier photos hadn't been faked. But he wouldn't have wanted the Bigfoot hunted down and caged. Would her father hide the bones and protect the creatures in the end?

The hair lifted on the back of her neck. She straightened slowly and turned, positive someone was watching her. In the trees, a pine bough moved. She heard the rustle of leaves followed by the snap of a limb, then silence.

She let go of the breath she'd been holding. No one there, she told herself. Just forest sounds. But she couldn't shake the feeling that not only wasn't she alone, but someone was very close by, watching her, waiting.

But waiting for what? Her to find the bones? Or evidence that her father's fall hadn't been an accident?

FORD LOST Rozalyn's tracks just before he reached the rimrocks. Earlier the rain had fallen in a steady drizzle, the low clouds offering little light. Even now that the rain had stopped, the air was damp, everything dripped and he could hear water cascading down the rocks off to his right not far from a huge old Douglas fir. The cliffs loomed ahead of him. Rozalyn would already be at the base of them. Might have already found a cave to explore.

He found himself running to catch up to her. As he topped a rise, he spotted her just yards away standing at the base of the rock cliff.

Something caught his eye higher up the cliff. A movement on a wide ledge directly above her. A dark figure clad in a raincoat, the hood up, bent over behind a large boulder. In the time it took for his heart to beat, Ford saw the boulder tumble off the edge of the cliff headed right for Rozalyn.

Chapter Twelve

Charity stepped into the *Timber Falls Courier* newspaper office and closed the door behind her, bracing herself for a tongue-lashing.

Daisy Dennison looked up when she heard Charity enter. She set down the newspaper, pulled a tissue from the box on Charity's desk and dried her tears as if ashamed to be caught crying.

Charity watched her, surprised how good the woman looked considering she'd been shot in the shoulder just two weeks before and had spent the past twenty-seven years a recluse in her mansion before that.

Daisy had gained some weight, had color again in her cheeks and had put some expensive highlights in her hair. She looked damned good, and Charity couldn't help but wonder if getting rid of Wade wasn't responsible for it more than anything else. Tears and all, Daisy looked happier than Charity had ever seen her.

Charity went to the small fridge next to the bathroom and opened the door. "Can I get you anything to drink?'' This definitely called for a Diet Coke—if not something stronger.

Daisy suddenly seemed to realize that she was sitting in Charity's chair and quickly got up. ''No, thank you. I…'' She took another wipe at her tears. ''I just need to talk to you.''

''If you came here to defend Wade—''

''No,'' Daisy said almost too quickly. ''It's…I'm worried. You don't know Wade like I do. You don't know what he's capable of.''

But Daisy did? ''If you're worried about my safety—''

''I'm worried about my own,'' the older woman snapped. Her eyes filled with tears again. ''I'm afraid he's going to snap and…and kill me.''

Charity stared at her, speechless.

''He blames me for everything,'' Daisy said, her voice breaking. ''For the rumors about the baby…'' Daisy looked away. ''I think in his mind he believes that Angela would never have been kidnapped if I hadn't…''

''Had an affair?'' Charity suggested.

Daisy's gaze swept back to hers, the eyes now cold and hard. ''This town is good for nothing *but* rumors. The baby was Wade's. There was never any doubt.''

''Are you sure about that?'' The moment the words were out of her mouth, Charity regretted them.

Daisy reached for her purse, anger giving her cheeks high color as she glared at Charity. ''I thought I could appeal to you as another woman and ask you not to do any more stories about this. Just let it be forgotten. Let us try to get on with our lives.''

She had to be kidding. "How is that possible, Daisy, when you still don't know what really happened to Angela? What about justice? Surely you don't think it's been done."

"Life isn't always just," Daisy said lifting her nose into the air. Except now everyone in town knew Daisy was no aristocrat. "Isn't it enough that the man who took my daughter is burning in hell as we speak?"

"Is it enough for you?" Charity asked.

Something dark flickered in the woman's gaze before she turned and left. She didn't even bother to slam the door.

Charity stared after her, wondering what Daisy had really come to see her about. It wasn't to ask her not to run any more stories. Daisy wasn't that naive.

No, Daisy Dennison had another agenda and Charity wondered what it was.

ROZ FIRST HEARD THE tinkle of small pebble-size rocks trickling down the cliff. Then a rumble. If she hadn't been standing under a rock face she might have thought it was thunder.

Rock slide!

She was too far from the trees to find safety there. Her only hope was a small cave back under the cliff face. Her feet were already moving as the first boulder careened down from overhead, showering her in dirt and rock chips before it thudded to the ground just inches from her. Overhead, she heard more boulders break loose and rumble downward.

As she dove for the shallow cave, she was hit hard from behind, the air knocked out of her as she was thrown to the ground just inside the mouth of the small dark cavern and rolled back under the overhang, something heavy coming to rest on her.

The earth shook as rocks pounded the ground next to her in a shower of crashing thunder that drowned out everything else except the sound of heavy breathing next to her ear and the weight on top of her.

The rocks seemed to fall forever. Then silence.

"You're crushing me," she wheezed into the chilling silence that followed the rock slide. She would know that distinct male scent anywhere, as well as the now familiar contours of his body. "You just can't stay off of me, can you?"

He rolled from her and she gasped for breath, flipping over to stare in shock at the pile of rocks in the spot where she'd been standing only moments before. She began to shake at the realization of just how close a call it had been and looked over at Ford.

He'd moved to a sitting position against the wall of the cliff. The look on his face surprised her, a combination of anger and—fear. "You *are* crazy," he spat. "What does it take to get through that thick skull of yours that this is dangerous?"

She glared at him. "The only danger I'm in is from you."

He shook his head in disgust. "*I'm* the one who keeps rescuing you."

"Really? And why is that?" she demanded.

"I was just asking myself that very question. Obviously not to impress you, that's for sure." He cautiously crawled from under the overhang, then reached back to grab her hand and pull her out behind him. He dragged her away from the cliff before he spun around to face her.

"What the hell are you doing up here by yourself? Do you realize you were almost killed? And worse, *I* was almost killed."

"It's what you get for following me," she snapped. "And don't try to tell me you saved my life again. I was jumping out of the way when you tackled me."

"I'm not going to try to tell you anything." He swore. "I should wash my hands of you. Let you get killed."

"If you're trying to scare me again—"

"Lady, if you were a cat, you'd be out of lives by now," he said, dusting himself off.

"I know the truth about you," she threw at him, remembering what she'd found at the guest house in the papers he'd tried to hide under his laptop, and what Charity had told her about him being in town two weeks ago.

"Yeah, I gathered that when you took off on me," he said and turned his back on her as he started toward the cliff face again.

"Why were you in town two weeks ago and failed to mention it? Where are you going? Aren't you even going to try to deny why you're really in town?" she demanded to his retreating backside.

"What would be the point?" He started to climb up a series of rocklike steps. "You coming or not?"

"What? And let you get me up there so you can push me off?"

"Don't tempt me. I thought you might be interested to know how those rocks just happened to fall."

Rock slides happened all the time in this part of the country. "Don't try to tell me that rock slide was anything but an accident."

He stopped and turned to look back at her. "And waste my breath? I'm going to show you. Unless you're afraid to climb up here."

Was that a *dare?* Did he really think she would fall for something so obvious as a dare? She glanced up at the cliff. She certainly wasn't afraid of climbing up there. But what would be the point? Just to prove the rock slide had been an accident? Just to prove him wrong?

She clambered up the cliff behind him wondering how he thought he could prove it was anything more than a rock slide when she and Ford were the only two people for twenty miles.

As she reached the wide ledge where he was waiting for her, she saw the smug look on his face. He'd known all he had to do was dare her and she'd climb up here. But she realized that wasn't the only reason for his smugness. He pointed to one clear boot print in a patch of wet earth in a flat rock at his feet. Past it there were scrape marks where a boulder had been pushed to the rim of the ledge.

Her heart caught in her throat as she spotted something else near one of the rocks along the ledge. She stepped closer and bent down. She heard Ford move to her side, heard him swear under his breath.

"Don't touch it," he ordered. He shrugged off his backpack, removed a small plastic container and carefully scooped up the two fresh cigarette butts where someone had smoked while they waited. From this point, a person would have had a clear view of the path below—the same one she'd just come up. ''The lab might be able to get DNA from a saliva sample.''

She nodded. She still had her camera strapped to her chest. She took it out and, stilling the trembling in her hands, turned back to get a shot of the single boot track in the mud. The tread was worn along the outside edge and she thought she might be able to match it if she ever came across the boot that had made it.

''You can't be serious,'' Ford said obviously realizing what she was thinking as he watched her take the photograph of the boot print. ''This person just tried to kill you—and probably put your father in the hospital. Unless you only plan to turn that photograph over to the sheriff—''

''Whoever did this doesn't know me,'' she said as she put her camera back into its case strapped to her chest. ''If this is the same person who hurt my father, I'm going to find him or die trying.''

''Exactly.'' He reached for her but she stepped away. His hand brushed hers. He felt her stiffen, saw the panic in her gaze. She'd felt it, too, the heat, the electricity, the heart-pounding, brain-numbing chemistry.

''You aren't going to try to stop me, are you?'' She didn't bother to give him time to reply. ''No, you want me to find the bones so you can make a name for yourself. Or is it the money you're after? Or both?''

"Would it do me any good to tell you you're wrong?"

"None," she said stepping over to the edge of the cliff, her back to him. She could see another storm coming, the sky dark, the rain headed this way. A light breeze came up out of the forest below them scented with cedar.

He cursed under his breath.

"Tell me, is this still your best behavior, because I'm having trouble telling."

ROZ STARED DOWN at the pile of stones, ignoring Ford as best she could. Her heart was pounding and she felt weak at just his touch. What was wrong with her? He was the enemy. The man was despicable. He would sell his soul for money and fame. And yet her body ached for his touch.

She turned, realizing the would-be killer had gotten down from here without being seen after the rock slide. So where had he gone?

She looked past Ford to a crack in the cliff and walked over to it, ignoring him. He was watching her, studying her, a frown on his face. The crack in the rock was just wide enough for a person to slip through. Beyond it she could see where the boot prints had slid down the earthy slope to a stand of trees.

What she couldn't understand was why her father would have ever come up here. Unless… She turned and looked down the ledge to where a tree grew out of the rocks. Behind it was darkness. A cave.

As she moved to it, she could see that it wasn't

very large, no more than three feet across, maybe six feet deep and about her height. It was hidden behind the tree unless you were standing at the right spot to see it. She would never have noticed it had she not been trying to determine where her assailant had gone.

She peered inside with her flashlight. The cave floor was smooth, rocky, no sign of digging. Nor any sign of bones embedded in the rock. It would have been too easy to find the bones here but she still couldn't hide her disappointment.

"What is it going to take to get through to you?" Ford asked impatiently behind her as the first drops of rain began to fall, splashing down hard on the rock ledge. She stood under the shelter of the pine tree but Ford stayed out in the rain, not seeming to notice it.

She turned, surprised how close he was. "You don't give a damn about me or my dad. That stunt at the hospital, getting Jesse Tanner to guard him night and day, was just a way to get to me. For all I know you set up everything—all the times you supposedly saved my life—including this one." She sounded close to tears and hated it.

His sea-green gaze washed over her in a warm wave. "Is that *really* what you think?" he asked quietly.

"Damn right it is," she said but her words carried little conviction and they both knew it. "You're an impossible man," she whispered, all the fight gone out of her. "Totally incorrigible."

"I've been told that on more than one occasion,"

he said as he stepped under the tree with her to thumb away an errant tear from her cheek.

The rough brush of his thumb pad sent a tremor quaking through her. She felt her pulse jump, her heart suddenly a drum in her chest. "What makes you such an ass one minute and such a...a..."

"A prince of a guy the next?" he asked. He was so close she swore she could feel heat radiating from his body. He looked down into her eyes. "I don't know. You probably have some theories though."

She let out the breath she'd been holding as she tried to step back, tried to put some distance between them, but there was no place to go. Her back was to rock. If she moved she would be forced into the cave. He had her trapped and he knew it.

"Don't," Rozalyn whispered. Her brown eyes swam with tears as she looked up at him. She drew in a short, shuddery breath. "Don't do this."

"And hate myself the rest of my life?" He touched her hair, not surprised that it felt as silken as it looked as he cupped her chin in his hand and turned her face up to his. Her eyes pleaded with him not to kiss her as he lowered his mouth to hers.

She seemed to hold her breath as if afraid to breathe, afraid to move. Her palms came up as if to push him away, but only rested against his chest as he deepened the kiss.

She groaned softly against his mouth, leaning into the kiss, leaning into him.

He tried to warn himself. This was crazy. If he didn't stop, there would be no turning back. But even as he thought it, he knew he'd gone way past the point of no return a long time ago with Rozalyn Sawyer. This felt as if it had always been written in the stars. As if he had spent his life headed for this moment— and nothing could stop the inevitable.

He knew he should run like hell. But running was the last thing he wanted to do right now. Think of the bones, the money, the scientific recognition. The fame.

"I want to make love to you," he heard himself say even though he knew instinctively he would be giving up both the money and the fame should they find the bones. He had a lot more to lose and he was putting it all on the line for the first time in his life. He'd never been so scared or so certain.

Roz lifted her hands from his chest as if to ward him off. He caught both in his and drew her hard against him.

His Caribbean-blue gaze locked with hers as he dropped his mouth to her lips. She felt herself diving into his gaze as if it really was tropical surf. It was heavenly. She kissed him back with a passion she hadn't known she even possessed.

A moan escaped his lips. He backed her up against the cool stone, pinning her there with the hard planes of his body. His mouth explored hers as his hands cupped her bottom and rain fell in a torrent just beyond the shelter of the tree. She'd never been kissed like this. In fact, she'd never known a kiss could have this effect.

She couldn't breathe. Her pulse boomed in her ears louder than thunder. He kissed her harder, his hands moving sensually up over her hips, over her breasts, her neck, to bury his fingers in her hair. He robbed her of her breath. Stole her good sense.

She melted against him as the rain pounded the rock ledge.

He pulled back, blew out a breath, his gaze locked with hers. "Tell me this isn't what you want."

She shook her head. She wanted this and more, so much more. She wanted to be naked with him, to make love with him. Crazy or not, she wanted to sleep with the enemy.

The rain fell harder. He dragged her down and into the cave, his mouth never leaving hers as he drew her to the floor of the cave and lay down beside her.

Her hand went to his cheek, his beard rough to her touch and she looked into all that sea-green and felt herself sinking deeper and deeper. There would be no coming up for air. Her life would never be the same after this.

"Do you trust me?" he whispered against her mouth.

She didn't want him to stop kissing her. Not now. She tried to draw him closer, but he pulled back to look at her. "Do you trust me?"

She gazed into his eyes, afraid of her answer. She looked deep and realized with a start that she did. Tears stung her eyes. She trusted him. God help her.

He smiled then. How had she not thought him handsome? He was glorious when he smiled and he was smiling at her as if he'd never seen anything he wanted more.

She wrapped her arms around his neck and drew him down until his lips were on hers, amazed the way he made her feel. Amazed even more by the words that came out of her mouth. "I want you to make love to me, Ford Lancaster."

He seemed to breathe a sigh of relief as he drew her closer and kissed her senseless, his hands roving over her body, sending shafts of heat to her center. He freed the top button of her blouse, his gaze never leaving hers. "If you change your mind, all you have to do is tell me to stop."

He slipped another button free. His fingertips brushed her skin, making her quiver inside. "Just say the word."

She swallowed hard. Her skin ached. She could feel her nipples, hard and tender against the sheer fabric of her bra. Just say the word. Any word and he would stop. She didn't utter a word, deathly afraid he *would* stop.

She closed her eyes, leaned her head back. She felt her blouse slip from her shoulders, felt his fingertips skim over the thin fabric of her bra and the hardened tips of her nipples beneath. She groaned and pressed against his mouth as it dropped to envelop one nipple, then the other.

His fingers were at the zipper of her jeans. She opened her eyes, a flash of rational thought. Say the word. Any word. Now. Or never.

She opened her mouth as his head came up from her breast but his gaze held a kind of wonder as he looked down at her and left her speechless.

Her heart drummed like the rain beating the rocks just outside the security of the cave as she made love with him.

Naked and in his arms, he released a well of passion from within her she hadn't even known existed. No man had ever touched her like that nor had she ever wanted to explore a man's body the way she did Ford's. It was as if there was nothing between them, no secrets, no boundaries. It was as if she'd found her way to a home she hadn't known existed. And when he'd pleasured her beyond her wildest dreams, she lay spent in his arms, tears of joy in her eyes. Whatever tomorrow might bring, she would never have regrets. In her heart, she knew it was meant to be.

WHEN ROZ opened her eyes, her body still alive with his touch, Ford was gone. She sat up and looked out of the cave, surprised how late it was. The rain had stopped. For a moment, she thought he'd taken off. It wouldn't have surprised her.

She pulled on her clothes and slipped out of the cave. Ford was just climbing up over the rim of the cliff about fifty yards away. She walked along the edge of the ledge to meet him.

Her body already ached for his touch. She was almost to him when she saw his grim expression. "You're sorry, aren't you?"

He seemed surprised by the question. "You mean about you and me?" His eyes seemed more blue than green in the dying light of day. He shook his head. "Never." He stepped to her and pulled her into his arms, cradling the back of her head in his large hand as he pressed her close.

Relief made her weak. She rested her cheek against his chest, listened to his beating heart. She knew he hadn't wanted to feel anything for her—just as she hadn't for him. What they felt was overwhelming and impossible to explain. And she suspected it scared him as much as it did her.

She looked out over the rainforest, then down to the rocks below, and suddenly tensed.

Ford turned her, trying to shield her from the sight. But it was too late. She'd seen her father's backpack lying in the dirt a dozen yards below them. "Oh, God, this can't be from where he fell."

"It isn't," Ford said, clasping her upper arms to keep her from stepping around him to take another look.

She struggled to free herself, but Ford's grip was strong, his will even stronger. He was determined to protect her. Damn him.

"Don't lie to me. Not now," she cried in frustration.

"Rozalyn, listen to me. Your father was never up here."

She stopped struggling and stared at him. "That's his backpack."

"Someone tried to make it look like Liam fell from up here, okay?" Ford said. "But he couldn't have. He would have landed closer to the cliff if he'd fallen. Or been pushed."

"You've been down there?"

He nodded. "There's blood down there on the rocks. Probably your father's but it was planted there. Do you understand what I'm staying? I've spent my life investigating elaborate hoaxes and exposing the offenders. I know what I'm doing."

"You were wrong about my father's photographs," she snapped.

He winced as if she'd slapped him and his eyes grew as dark as the depths of the ocean. "What is it you want me to say? That I've been an ass most of my thirty-six years? All right, you've got it. You think all my motives are self-seeking, maybe they are. Maybe I'm kidding myself that they're not anymore. Maybe a person can't change. Especially me."

Afternoon shadows lengthened under the pines below them and the air cooled perceptively. She felt confused, afraid and angry with him. For a while she'd forgotten who he was back there in the cave. Or why he was here with her now. "If you're looking for sympathy—"

He laughed. "You're a tough one. You aren't going to cut me any slack at all, are you? Okay," he said holding up a palm to hush her before she could say anything. "I'm up here just for the money and the glory. But your father still didn't fall from this cliff. Nor was he pushed. All of this," he said waving his hand through the air, "was *staged*. Liam wasn't found up here. Whoever dropped him off at the hospital was the person who put him in the coma. This isn't about Bigfoot bones. I doubt it ever was."

"But the doctor said some Bigfoot hunters dropped him at the hospital," she said.

Ford nodded. "I know. That's why we have to get to the hospital as quickly as possible."

Chapter Thirteen

Once off the mountain, Ford followed Rozalyn in his pickup as far as the edge of town where she left her SUV. On the way to the hospital, he told her what he'd found at Lost Creek Falls earlier that morning.

She turned the piece of painted plastic mannequin face over in her fingers for a long time without saying a word. "I'm not crazy."

"No. What I can't figure out is why someone would do this," he said. "It was obviously planned specifically for you. Whoever did it anticipated your reaction. They had to have known about your mother's suicide, had to know you would risk your life to save the person you thought was about to jump."

"Drew told me his mother resented me and he was afraid she might have been pulling some tricks on me, trying to keep me away from Timber Falls so my father would let them move somewhere and start over fresh."

"What kind of tricks?" He listened while she told him about the phonograph.

Then he said, "Before I went to the waterfall, I

dropped the sample you gave me last night at the lab. The results were positive. It's a drug used by doctors to help induce hypnosis in patients and has the same symptoms as sleepwalking. The person under the drug is very susceptible to suggestion.''

She hugged herself, biting down on her lower lip. ''Someone talked me up into the attic and out onto the widow's walk?''

''It certainly would appear so.''

''Drew?''

''I doubt Drew would have left the note if he'd been the one to drug the chocolates,'' Ford said.

Anyone in the house could have known about what time Rozalyn would be coming up the road. He sighed. ''If Emily is behind this, she's doing more than just trying to scare you away. And what bothers me is Liam's accident. He obviously was attacked somewhere else and his assailant didn't want anyone to know where.''

''Why, if not because of Bigfoot bones?'' she asked.

All Liam had said was bones. But what other kind of bones were there?

Human bones.

Ford sped up the SUV.

''I just don't understand why the person who attacked my father would take him to the hospital,'' she said.

''To be able to tell the story about him being found under the cliff and take away any suspicion,'' he said. And to make sure he died, Ford thought as he turned down the street toward the hospital, tires screeching.

Roz had Liam's backpack in her lap. She'd been going through it and looked worried and scared. "The digital camera isn't in the pack. But the usual things he always takes on his day trips like his GPS and binoculars are."

"Maybe the camera was stolen from the backpack before we got there."

"But the thief would leave a GPS and a pair of expensive binoculars." She shook her head. "I don't think the digital camera was ever in here." She turned to stare out the window, looking as scared as he felt.

"Who told you that your father had gone up into the mountains?"

"Emily, when I called the house."

"Your father has money. Who gets it if something happens to him?" Ford asked.

She stared at him. "My father insisted Emily sign a prenuptial agreement with me getting the bulk of his estate."

He nodded. "And if anything happens to you?"

"Since I'm not married and have no children it would go to…my father's wife, I guess," Rozalyn said.

Ford nodded as he swung into the hospital parking lot.

WHEN SHERIFF Mitch Tanner returned to his office, the information he'd been awaiting was on his desk.

All of Wade Dennison's and Bud Farnsworth's financial records from twenty-eight years ago. He sat down in his chair, surprised the express package wasn't thicker. Then again, twenty-eight years ago,

Wade was just starting out, Dennison Ducks had only begun to establish a name for itself in the decoy world and Wade and Daisy had only been married three years. Even though Daisy had spent Wade's money as if there was no tomorrow back then, there wasn't the wealth there was now—or the paperwork.

Mitch's cell phone rang. He almost didn't answer it, anxious to see what he'd find in the finances of the two men. "Hello?"

"Mitch, it's Charity."

As if he didn't know that. Just the sound of her voice warmed him in a way that could only get him into trouble. He couldn't believe he'd suggested they move in together. Actually, he'd been just short of suggesting something much more permanent. Thank God, Roz had shown up when she did.

"I need a huge favor. Would you run the name Lynette Hargrove for me," she said. "I need it ASAP."

"Of course you do," he said and thought about arguing that his computer wasn't for the use of nosy reporters but that would have taken more time than just typing in the name. He moved the financial package aside. "Spell it for me."

Lynette Hargrove. He curbed his curiosity. Even if Charity told him the real reason she wanted the name run, which was doubtful, it would be a long, involved explanation because it was Charity. He'd just wait and see what came up on the computer screen.

"It's going to take a few minutes," he said glancing toward the package. "Can I get back to you?"

"Promise?"

"Promise."

She hung up before he did. That was odd. Not like Charity at all. He sighed and reached for the package.

As he tore it open and pulled out the papers, he put Charity's call out of his mind.

"You need anything else before I call it a day?" Sissy asked from the doorway.

He didn't look up, just shook his head and after a moment, the clerk closed the door. He knew she was dying to know what was in the package from the bank. So was he.

It didn't take long to find the first large cash withdrawal made from Wade and Daisy Dennison's personal joint checking account. Ten thousand dollars.

Mitch unlocked his desk drawer, pulled out the Angela Dennison file and flipped through it until he found her birth date. May eighth. The first withdrawal was made on August thirtieth the previous year. Like clockwork, there was a withdrawal on the thirtieth of each month. The final withdrawal was made on April thirtieth—just days before the kidnapping and unlike the others, it was for twenty thousand, for a total of one hundred thousand dollars.

"Hot damn," Mitch swore as he leaned back in his chair. "One hundred thousand dollars." He thought about the shopping trips Daisy used to take. The expensive horses Wade bought her. All of that seemed to be accounted for. This hundred thousand wasn't.

He picked up Bud Farnsworth's bank records telling himself Bud wouldn't be stupid enough to put the money in the bank.

Wrong. There it was, deposited each month just a couple of days after the money left the Dennison's private account.

"Oh man, Charity was right." Wouldn't she love to know that? She'd said all along that Bud Farnsworth never would have come up with the kidnapping idea by himself. Still, it was circumstantial evidence and Mitch was sure Wade would try to explain it away. But there was little doubt that Bud Farnsworth had been paid to kidnap Angela Dennison.

The bad feeling hit him like a brick almost doubling him over. All this information had been there twenty-eight years ago. It would have been even easier for Mitch's predecessor, his mentor, the man he'd spent his life trying to emulate. One of the first things Sheriff "Hud" Hudson would have done was check the bank records.

Mitch swore, sick at even the thought that Hud could have been bought off. It wasn't possible. So why hadn't this come out all those years ago? Why not until now?

Was it possible that Wade had accounted for the money? Is that why nothing had ever come of it?

He glanced up at the computer screen, having forgotten his promise to Charity. The information on half a dozen Lynette Hargroves had come through.

Frowning, he clicked on a link to a newspaper article about a Lynette Hargrove who'd been a nurse in Timber Falls ten years ago. That caught his attention. She was wanted for questioning in the disappearance of the doctor she'd been employed by at the time—

Dr. James Morrow, a doctor who specialized in hypnosis.

He clicked on another link. Lynette Hargrove had been killed, her body burned beyond recognition after her car left the highway and rolled near Portland. The article said she had been wanted for questioning in a missing person's case. He looked for newspaper articles on Dr. Morrow. As far as Mitch could tell, Dr. Morrow had never been found.

This had to be the Lynette Hargrove that Charity was interested in. He wondered what Charity's interest was. It was better than thinking about Sheriff Hudson. Could Mitch have been that wrong about the man?

Why was Lynette's name coming up now after all these years? After Ford Lancaster had asked him to check Anna Sawyer's case file? After Mitch had seen that Lynette Hargrove had been questioned by the former sheriff about Dr. Morrow's visit to Anna Sawyer just before her suicide? Lynette had said she knew nothing about the visit, that she hadn't even been in town.

His phone rang. He flipped it on without looking to see who was calling, expecting it was Charity. "I hadn't forgotten to call you." A lie.

"Sheriff, it's dispatch. I have an urgent call from Daisy Dennison."

He sat up, surprised as Daisy was connected and he heard fear in her voice.

"Wade just phoned me. He sounded as if he'd been drinking. He said he was on his way up here. He…he threatened to kill me and I'm afraid—"

"Lock your doors, I'm on my way," Mitch said, as he dumped everything into the drawer, locked it and took off for the Dennison house.

FORD THREW OPEN his car door and ran toward the emergency room entrance, Rozalyn at his heels. *Let me be wrong. Please, let this be one of those times I'm wrong.*

But he couldn't shake the bad feeling that twisted his insides.

Rain pounded the pavement. A breeze stirred the nearby trees emitting a low moan. Chilled, Ford pushed open the door, hoping to see that nice older nurse at her station.

The nurse's station was empty. No lights had been turned on yet, making the hallway dark. An eerie quiet moved ghostlike through the place.

Ford broke into a run again. As he burst through the door to Liam's hospital room, the first thing he saw was a water glass on its side on a dinner tray at Jesse's feet—the food on the tray floated in a sea of pink as a blob of red gelatin slowly melted.

Jesse was in his chair, slumped, chin to chest, his feet at an odd angle.

Ford's gaze shot past him to Liam lying on the bed. A startled Dr. Harris turned in surprise from where he stood over his patient, the pillow he'd just lifted off Liam's face still in his hands.

Ford didn't break stride as he dove across the bed at Harris. He hit the doctor chest high, driving him into the wall. The pillow fell to the floor as Ford punched the doctor in the face with an uppercut that put the man's lights out.

As Dr. Harris slid down the wall to the floor, Ford swung around to check Liam, afraid he was too late.

Liam's eyes were open, unblinking.

Ford swore and threw back his head, wanting to howl out his pain. He'd failed Rozalyn. Failed.

At a sound behind him, he swung around expecting to find Rozalyn in the doorway. Nurse Kate Clark blinked in confusion, a box of donuts in her hands.

"Call the sheriff, hurry," Ford barked as he ripped off his belt and grabbed some tubing from the tray next to the bed and began to tie up the doctor.

Kate dropped the donuts and picked up the phone in the room, fingers trembling as she beat out 9-1-1.

Ford heard Jesse groan in the corner. Kate was on the phone with the dispatcher. The sheriff was on a call, Kate told Ford. The dispatcher would get word to him as soon as she could.

Ford looked to the hospital room doorway. Still no Rozalyn. She must have seen Dr. Harris holding the pillow over her dad's face, must have known they were too late and taken off in her grief.

And yet, even as Ford thought it, a part of him knew she wouldn't do that. He hurriedly finished tying up the doctor, anxious to find her and comfort her, upset with himself, afraid for her. Why the hell would Harris want Liam Sawyer dead? It didn't make any sense. If he hadn't seen the doctor holding the pillow over Liam's face—

And hadn't been suspect of the doctor's story that Liam had been dropped off at the hospital by some out-of-town Bigfoot hunters.

"The doctor sent you to get donuts?" Ford asked

the nurse as she hung up the phone and reached to take Liam's pulse.

She nodded distractedly. ''He said he should have gotten something to eat when he brought the tray for Jesse, but that he craved jelly-filled donuts and could I—''

''What the hell?'' Jesse said as he looked over at the doctor on the floor, then tried to sit up and doubled over to be sick.

''Kate, did you see Rozalyn when you came in?'' Ford asked as he finished securing Dr. Harris. ''Did you see which way she went?''

Behind Ford, Jesse struggled to his feet and seemed to take in the situation quickly. ''Son of a bitch. The bastard drugged me.''

''Did you see Rozalyn, Kate?''

The nurse shook her head. Her gaze transfixed on Liam.

Ford reached across the bed to get her attention. Bony fingers closed over his wrist.

''You look like John,'' said a raspy voice from the bed.

Ford blinked, then focused on Liam and the hand gripping his wrist.

''Where is Roz?'' Liam whispered.

Ford shook his head in disbelief, then turned, hoping again to see her standing there. ''Rozalyn!'' No answer. ''Rozalyn!''

''I saw her on my way in,'' Kate said.

And Ford breathed a sigh of relief.

''Find Roz. Not Emily,'' Liam whispered and Kate

gave him a little water, his lips dry and chapped. "Lynette."

Ford frowned down at the man. Who was Lynette? Liam wasn't making any sense.

The old man was frantic now, gripping Ford's arm. "They'll...kill her. The...bones." He fell back, exhausted, his fingers falling away from Ford's wrist.

"I knew it!" cried a thin female voice from the doorway.

Ford swung around to find an elderly woman in a bright-colored caftan, her red hair piled high on her head, turquoise eye shadow over shining blue eyes, standing in the doorway. "Do you know what he's talking about?"

"Emily. You fool. She's really Lynette Hargrove and she's a killer!" the woman said rushing to Liam's side.

"Florie Jenkins," Jesse said by way of introduction. "She's harmless. Thinks she's psychic."

"I'm *clairvoyant*," Florie said, cradling Liam's hand in both of her jeweled ones. "The woman was only after Liam's money. Don't just stand there," she snapped at Ford. "Your destiny is with Rozalyn and I just saw her leaving."

Kate's eyes widened. "When I saw her she was talking to her stepbrother Drew in the hallway—"

Chapter Fourteen

Charity found herself pacing. Mitch hadn't called back about Lynette Hargrove. That wasn't like him. Maybe there was nothing to find. Or maybe there was something. Something he didn't want to see in print. That was more likely.

She started to pick up the phone and call Mitch. Instead, she dialed one of the two numbers she'd gotten from the Portland directory. Neither line had answered earlier, not that she'd expected them to since Drew and Suzanne were both in Timber Falls.

The number for Drew Lane rang and rang. She started to hang up, wondering why she didn't just call Mitch when a young male voice said, "Hello?" He sounded breathless.

"Andrew Lane?" Charity asked incredulously.

"Yes?" Now he sounded suspicious.

"I'm sorry. I'm trying to find the attorney's son."

"My father is deceased."

"I'm not sure I have the right Andrew Lane. You have a sister Suzanne?"

"Yes?" More suspicion in his voice.

"Just tell me this. Has your mother Emily remarried?"

"No," he said. "What is this about?"

"I do have the wrong number. Sorry." Charity hung up with fingers shaking, as she quickly dialed Roz's cell phone. Out of the area or turned off. Charity felt cold inside and scared. What were the chances that there was another hotshot attorney named Andrew Lane with a wife named Emily and two grown children named Andrew and Suzanne? None. Nada. Nil.

Liam's new wife hadn't just passed herself off as Emily Lane, she'd brought along two offspring. Hers? Or had she just borrowed them from some actor's school?

And the big question: Why?

For Liam Sawyer's money just as Florie had suspected.

Frantically, Charity started to dial Mitch's number but then she saw his patrol car go racing by.

Charity grabbed her purse and ran out to her car in hot pursuit.

THE LIGHTS of the patrol car cut through the darkness as Mitch raced up to the Dennison house. It was a huge house with white pillars, a Southern mansion in the wilds of Oregon. Wade had built it for his young wife. Off to the back were stables from when Wade had bought Daisy expensive horses. Directly behind the house was a large indoor pool and recreation room larger than any hotel.

The last time Mitch had been out here, the drapes

had been drawn and he'd had to force Daisy Dennison to come to the door. She'd been a recluse for twenty-seven years. That was until a woman named Nina Monroe had come to town with a secret. Since then, Daisy seemed to have come back to life, kicking Wade out and, if local rumors were right, talking about filing for divorce, both of which had obviously set her husband off.

And that's what worried Mitch as he noticed this visit the drapes were open, all the lights on and the front door was standing ajar. The four-car carport off to the right was also open and empty except for Daisy's SUV.

On the way through town, Mitch had seen Desiree Dennison's little red sports car parked in front of the Duck Inn bar. Today was the maid's day off. She always went to Portland on her day off and was a creature of habit like none other Mitch had ever seen.

That meant Daisy had been alone.

Mitch swore as he parked beside Wade's Ford Navigator, got out and started up the wide steps to the veranda.

"Daisy? Wade? It's Sheriff Tanner." No answer.

He stepped into the foyer, broken glass grating under his shoe sole. A pane of glass from the front door lay shattered on the floor.

Mitch drew his weapon and moved deeper into the house. In the living room, he saw the remains of what appeared to have been a struggle. An overturned chair. A lamp base crushed on the floor next to it. More glass and—

He froze, heart hammering. The wall was splattered

with what at first appeared to be blood. A broken wineglass lay on the floor in a puddle of red the same color as the spots on the wall. Mitch took a temporarily relieved breath.

"Daisy? Wade?" Still no answer. He continued through the lower floor of the house and had started up the wide staircase when he spotted the bright-colored scarf on the floor in front of a set of French doors that opened on the back of the house. Past it, he saw the lights were on in the pool house, shadows moving jerkily inside.

He ran to the pool house in time to hear the report of a gunshot echoing across the water. He didn't feel the pain until he was already pitching forward.

DREW PRESSED the hard, cold barrel of the gun against Roz's temple. "Stop here," he ordered.

She brought the sports car to a stop and leaned over the wheel, still fighting the heart-wrenching sobs that had made driving nearly impossible when he'd told her that her father was dead.

Drew reached over, turned off the engine and pocketed the key. A smothering darkness moved in quickly around them. The only sound was Roz sobbing softly.

"Come on."

She lifted her head, wiping her tears, anger stilling her sobs temporarily. It took a moment for her eyes to adjust. He'd forced her to drive to a spot along the far side of the house, hidden from both the guest house and the front driveway.

He grabbed a handful of her hair. "Get out. Go slow. I'm coming with you."

She opened her door. She'd already looked into his eyes, seen the bottomless coldness she'd glimpsed in Emily's eyes. It was what had convinced her to go quietly with him in the hospital.

Drew had come up behind her as she had stopped in her father's hospital room doorway. He'd motioned for her to be quiet or he would kill her, then he dragged her back away from the door making it clear he wouldn't just kill her but Ford also if she screamed or struggled.

She'd gone with him thinking Ford would be safe. Once in the car, Drew had told her that her father was dead. That Ford hadn't gotten there in time to save Liam from Dr. Harris, a friend of Drew's mother.

"Mother wants to see you," Drew said now as he slid out of the car behind her, still gripping a handful of her hair and pressing the gun barrel against her temple.

Roz hadn't said a word since Drew had forced her from the hospital and into his car. She'd cried but done as he ordered, all the time feeling the grief turn to rage.

As her eyes adjusted to the light, she could make out the crest of the house over the top of the trees. Drew let go of her hair to pull a flashlight from his jacket pocket. He gave it three short flashes, all pointed toward the house.

An instant later, a light came on in the attic near the widow's walk and Roz saw Emily waiting for them.

As MITCH fell to the pool house floor, the thick scent of chlorine filling his lungs, he saw Daisy and Wade on the other side of the lap pool struggling for the gun.

He saw the intensity of the struggle in Daisy's face just before he hit the tile floor hard. Pain shot up his side and he thought he would black out. "Put down the gun, Wade," he ordered weakly.

It was an idle threat as he watched his own weapon dislodge from his fingers and skitter across the tiles to come to rest under one of the lounge chairs.

Mitch tried to rise, realized it wasn't going to happen and rolled over onto his back. He clutched his side, his uniform shirt soaked with what he knew was his own blood.

Daisy was screeching now.

Another shot reverberated through the pool house. More pain. In his left leg this time. The screeching sound ended in a loud splash.

"Daisy?" His voice came out a hoarse whisper. He turned his head. He could see her in the water now, Wade standing over her on the edge of the pool on the other side, the gun in his hand.

"Wade, don't kill him!" Daisy cried as she surfaced and began to swim toward Mitch. "Kill me. That's why you came up here. Kill me!"

"Don't do it, Wade," Mitch said gritting his teeth against the pain. Tiny dark spots danced before his eyes and he willed himself not to pass out. "You okay, Daisy?" He could hear the lap of water next to him. "Daisy?"

"She's just fine," Wade said, his voice sounding

strange even to Mitch's ears. Closer than he'd expected, too. He was standing over Mitch, looking down at him. Wade's jacket bloomed with blood from a bullet hole, shoulder-high.

"Oh God, Wade, what have you done?" Daisy said weakly from the edge of the pool.

"Shut up," Wade bellowed, his voice echoing across the water as he swung the gun on her. "I *should* kill you. You shot me. You're trying to destroy me."

Daisy pushed a lock of wet hair back from her face and looked up at her husband with hatred in her eyes. "Destroy you?!" she screamed. "Destroy *you* after what you did to me?!"

"Shut up!" Wade bellowed and closed his eyes, grimacing as if in pain. "I loved you. I *loved* you."

Mitch caught movement behind Wade. His heart stopped as he saw Charity creep into the pool house unnoticed. She carefully picked up one of the oars that decorated the wall over the pool door.

"Take it easy, Wade," Mitch said, his voice raspy with pain. Neither Wade nor Daisy had seen Charity edging toward Wade with the oar. "You don't want to kill anyone."

Wade wagged his big head. "You think I shot you? That's what she wants you to think. She set me up. Told me to come to the house to talk about things and then pulled a gun on me and shot me."

"Wade, no one's going to believe that story," Daisy said, sounding tired and depressed. "Everyone in town knows your temper. I shot you to defend myself. You were trying to kill me."

He was shaking his head. "I *loved* you." His voice broke. He sounded close to tears. "I would have done anything for you. *Anything*. Even raised another man's child."

Mitch thought of his own mother and felt a chill as he looked at the venomous way Daisy glared at Wade. This is what he feared in a relationship. That love could turn to hate just like that.

Wade opened his eyes and pointed the gun at her head. She didn't even blink.

"Go ahead, Wade. Put me out of my misery. Do it. Kill me!" Daisy cried up at him. "You weak bastard. You can't even do that."

Charity swung the oar. Wade didn't know what hit him. The force of the blow dislodged the gun from his hand. It fell into the water as he went sailing out over the pool past Daisy, belly-flopping on the water and sending up a huge splash.

Mitch closed his eyes and lay back.

"Oh, Mitch." Charity was crying as she jerked off her shirt and wadded it up against the wound in his side. He could hear the sound of an ambulance and knew she had to have called when she heard the first shot. "You'd do anything to get out of marrying me."

He opened his eyes and tried to smile.

"Damn you, don't you even think about dying on me," she said tearfully. "I swear I'll track you down in heaven."

He managed to smile up at her. At least he thought he did. She looked beautiful. Especially without her shirt. Along with the sound of the ambulance, he could hear the sound of a motorcycle coming up the road, hell-bent. Jesse to the rescue. She'd called Jesse as well. What would he do without Charity? he wondered. He hoped he never had to find out.

He heard Wade come up sputtering from the deep end of the pool, all the fight gone out of him as he treaded water, his clothes billowing around him in the water.

Mitch glanced over at Daisy. She had disappeared under the water. He tried to sit up. Couldn't. Got out only the one word. "Gun."

Charity turned just as Daisy came up with the weapon Wade had dropped. She had it in both hands and was pointing the barrel end at Wade.

"I'm never going to have to fear you again," she said and pulled the trigger.

Wade didn't even try to duck the bullet. He just stared at her with a hurt look on his face as the bullet tore through the sleeve of his shirt and the flesh of his arm.

Charity dove into the water, coming up behind Daisy and grabbed her around the neck with one arm. As they struggled for the gun, Mitch called on every ounce of strength he had to drag himself over to the lounge chair, reach under it and come up with his gun.

He fired the shot in the air. "Drop the gun, Daisy. Now!" His voice boomed across the pool.

Daisy stilled. The weapon slipped from her fingers, made a faint splash, then floated slowly to the bottom of the pool. Charity released her hold on Daisy's neck as Jesse came racing in, took one look at the situation, pulled Mitch's weapon from his fingers and began giving orders.

Mitch lay back and closed his eyes again. He could smell Charity's perfume, feel her warm breath on his cheek, her wet hand brushing his hair back from his forehead. He was overwhelmed with his love for her. "Marry me."

Silence. "What?"

He opened his eyes and looked into hers. Any doubts he had about him and Charity were gone like a puff of smoke. In some cases, maybe love could conquer all. All he knew was that he couldn't go on living without this woman. "Marry me." Unfortunately, he blacked out before he heard her reply.

Roz LOOKED toward the house, her legs turning to water beneath her as she saw what Drew and Emily had planned for her. She'd been afraid at the hospital. Even more frightened in the car, thinking Drew was just going to take her out and shoot her. But now she knew that her death was to be exactly like her mother's. History was to repeat itself.

A tremor rattled through her. She fought back the terror that threatened to incapacitate her. She would die trying to avenge Liam Sawyer's death—and if she could, she would take Drew and his mother with her.

As Drew pushed her toward an opening in the dense garden behind the house, shining the flashlight beam a few feet in front of her, she wondered where Suzanne was. Hiding in a bottle or had that, too, just been an act? Was Suzanne waiting for her as well?

Three against one. The odds weren't good and Drew had a gun. Roz knew she would have to be very lucky to come out of this alive. She didn't feel lucky right now.

"Was it only for my father's money?" she asked as he pushed her down the garden path that wound toward the house while he held the gun to her back.

Drew laughed. "You think Mother cared anything about your father? The man wears flannel shirts and work boots. A man with that kind of money and he dresses like a mountain man not even to mention the difference in their ages."

"So your mother planned to kill —" her voice broke. She couldn't say "my dad" without crying "—Liam from the very first?"

"Isn't that what you've always suspected?" he sneered as he prodded her forward with the gun.

It surprised her that her feelings had been so transparent. The hate she heard in Drew's voice threatened her resolve to fight until the very end. She thought about making a run for it. She knew Drew would shoot her in the back. That seemed far better than what Emily had planned for her in the attic.

But it also seemed the coward's way out. Given a little time, maybe she could turn the tables on her new family.

Her greatest fear though was that Ford would realize she was gone and try to help her as usual. She couldn't stand the thought of Drew hurting him, let alone killing him. That's what worried her. That and a worse thought. That someone had been waiting in her father's room, waiting to take care of Ford. That meant something had happened to Jesse, as well.

She had never felt so alone. She stumbled, fighting

the horrible fear that, like her father, Ford was no longer alive. She couldn't bear the thought.

Drew shoved her again and she felt a cold, clear shot of anger race through her veins. He and his mother and sister weren't going to get away with this. She would bide her time. She would wait for an opening. She would try to keep a cool head and pray for a break.

And all this because her father had money and Emily and her family wanted it.

Roz must have said those words out loud because Drew snapped, "What would you know about being poor? Having nothing? You're a little rich girl."

She wanted to argue. Her parents hadn't lived extravagantly. Her father had never flaunted the money that had been handed down to him from past generations. If anything, he lived just the opposite and had taught Roz to live just as frugally. She'd never given much thought to the money she would someday inherit. She made her own money and lived just fine.

The thought made her angry. "Do you even have a job?"

"What? You think taking care of my mother isn't a full-time job?" Drew let out a laugh that held no humor. "You know nothing about me or my life."

How true. "Is your name even Drew Lane?" The silence chilled her. Could Florie be right? "My God, her name isn't Emily. She really is Lynette Hargrove." She heard his intake of air behind her and turned to see the answer in his startled expression.

He stepped past her to open the back door and shoved her inside. "What else do you know?"

Not near enough. "I know she faked her death in a car wreck." She stumbled into the house. It was dark except for a light over the back stairs. He pushed her toward the stairs. "And she had an affair with Dr. Morrow," Roz said, clutching at straws.

"One out of two isn't bad." He prodded her up the stairs. "You don't want to know. Trust me. It would be better to die not knowing."

She began to climb as slowly as possible, afraid he might be right. "Tell me."

"Okay, you asked for it."

She had almost reached the attic. Time was almost up.

"She killed the good doctor, Morrow, after he caught her stealing drugs."

Roz held her breath, knowing instinctively there was more.

"And the kicker? I helped her bury him in your garden," Drew said. "I was nine at the time."

"Oh, Drew," Roz said, unable to imagine the childhood he must have had.

"That wasn't the worst of it," he said. "Your mother saw us."

Chapter Fifteen

As Roz neared the attic, she heard the music coming from the phonograph and felt her blood run cold. It was her mother's favorite record. The one Roz had broken into bits just the night before.

But it was playing again now on the old phonograph.

It took all of her strength to take those last few steps up the stairs to the attic. No one had believed her about the voices she'd heard or that loud thud over her head.

If only she had gone upstairs to see what the noise had been. If only she hadn't convinced herself it was the wind. If only her mother had cried out for help.

No, she thought. Her mother wouldn't have because she knew there was only one other person in the house that day. Roz. But her mother must have argued with Emily, Lynette, whatever her name really was. That had been the voices she'd heard. And the loud thump?

She stumbled on the last stair as she remembered turning down her stereo but she hadn't been able to hear anything overhead because... Her heart lodged in her throat. Because her mother's phonograph had been playing so loudly.

Just as it was now. The same song.

Drew jabbed her in the ribs with the gun.

Roz did it without thinking, without even considering the consequences. She spun around, bringing her elbow back hard. It caught Drew in the face, blood instantly spurting from his nose as he cried out and grabbed for the stair railing. Except there wasn't any on the back stairs.

His eyes widened as he grabbed for her with the hand without the weapon. She slapped his hand away at the same moment the deafening boom of the gunshot echoed through the stairwell.

She waited for the pain in that instant as she watched Drew flail, then fall backward to tumble down the stairs as the sound of the gunshot died away. He crashed into the door at the bottom with a groan.

It took Roz a moment to realize she hadn't been shot.

Now! Get out of here! Run!

She looked down the steps. Drew was struggling to his feet, cursing and reaching for his dropped weapon. She couldn't get down there before he retrieved the gun. Nor could she get past him if she did.

The record stopped playing. There was a soft click. And then the needle dropped on the vinyl again.

Roz turned, knowing there was only one way out of here and that was the attic. A dark shadow filled the doorway.

"Rozalyn," Lynette Hargrove said, the gun in her

hand gleaming in the dim light. "So nice that you could make it but as always you've made a mess of things."

FORD DROVE as fast as his pickup would allow him, around the corners and up the lane to the front of the Sawyer house. Drew had Rozalyn. This was the logical place to bring her given what Ford had seen of Drew's relationship with his mother, whoever the hell she was.

The sky was black, rain drumming down in a thick dark veil. Ford figured the front door would be locked—not standing open. It was almost as if they'd been expecting him. Waiting for him.

He hoped to hell that meant Rozalyn was all right. He'd left word for the sheriff. Whatever Drew had planned for Rozalyn, it wasn't going to work. Liam was alive. The game was over. Ford just hoped once Drew knew that—

"Rozalyn!" he hollered as he raced up the porch steps and into the house. "Rozalyn!"

He heard music. Faint, but definitely coming from upstairs somewhere. It was an old song, one he couldn't quite place but he suspected it was the same song Rozalyn had told him about, her mother's favorite record.

The living room and dining room French doors were open, the rooms empty at a glance. He rushed up the stairs, taking them three at a time, as he followed the sound of the music.

He'd been so obsessed with Bigfoot bones, he hadn't thought the bones Liam had mentioned could be anything else. He'd done everything wrong, made so many mistakes. That's all he could think about as he cried out Rozalyn's name, not bothering to stop at the first or second-floor landings. His gut instinct told him where he'd find Rozalyn. In the attic.

The music played overhead as he clambered up the steps, no longer calling her name, afraid of what he would find. Or wouldn't find.

The panel at the end of the third floor was open—just as he knew it would be. He ran to it and bounded up the stairs.

As he reached the top and burst into the attic, he saw the old automatic phonograph sitting on the floor by the doorway. A single 45 spun on the turntable, the needle scratching across the record, the music coming out the tinny speakers.

In that instant, the song stopped, the phonograph moaned and groaned, then a soft click and the record began to play again.

Past the phonograph, he saw Rozalyn by the widow's walk. Only this time she wasn't alone.

"Come on in, Mr. Lancaster," Emily said. Except she wasn't Emily, right? She was some woman named Lynette Hargrove. "You're just in time."

"I've got some bad news, Lynette," Ford said as he moved into the room. He saw her react to the name. So the old broad at the hospital with the bright red hair knew what she was talking about. But that meant that Lynette was more dangerous than even he had suspected.

Lynette stood with a gun to Rozalyn's head. Next to her, Drew pressed a blood-soaked handkerchief to his nose with one hand and held a gun in the other. The barrel was pointed at the floor and he seemed distracted by his injuries, including a nasty gash on his forehead. Had Rozalyn given that to him? Drew looked as if he'd taken a bad fall. That was his girl, he thought with pride. Off to the right behind the couch, the young blond Suzanne was sprawled in a pool of her own blood, a bullet hole between her eyes, her sightless blue eyes staring up at the attic ceiling.

Ford hoped to God that Roz hadn't seen her, hadn't completely realized yet just what her stepmother was capable of.

"We already know the news," Lynette said over the sound of the phonograph playing next to him. "Liam is dead. Such a pity."

"Wrong," Ford was happy to inform her. "Liam is alive and conscious. In fact, he is talking to the sheriff at this very moment." A slight exaggeration. "And he's not the only one talking. Your boyfriend, Mark, Dr. Harris? He's talking as well."

Lynette turned the color of her bottle-blond hair. "That's a lie." The record stopped. The room was suddenly deathly quiet. Then the song began again.

"I stopped Dr. Harris from killing him." Ford's gaze went to Rozalyn. He nodded and smiled. "Your dad's fine. Conscious. He's tough. Like you." Ford looked into Rozalyn's eyes and liked what he saw. Anger in her gaze and a steeliness to her backbone that told him she was ready to kick butt if she only got the chance. He hoped to give them both the chance.

"Right now, Liam is telling the sheriff everything—including about the bones." Ford knew he really was clutching at straws now. For a moment he thought he might have made a mistake. All Liam had said was something about finding bones. But how did that tie in with this woman and her beyond dysfunctional family?

ROZ HAD NEVER been so happy—or so upset—to see anyone in her life. But having Ford here only made her more determined that they would get out of this alive. Ford had saved Liam. Her father was alive!

"Lynette killed and buried Dr. Morrow in our garden," she said, wondering how much Ford actually knew. From the look of gratitude she witnessed in his expression, not much. She filled Ford in about Lynette Hargrove and the stolen drugs. "My father must have found the bones."

"What was Dr. Morrow going to do? Have you arrested for stealing drugs?" Ford asked.

"Dr. Morrow had stopped by to see my mother that day. She and the doctor had become friends. He confided in her that he'd caught Lynette stealing drugs. He was a kind, caring man. He would have hated to have Lynette arrested because she was the single mother of a son. Lynette must have followed him when he left. She might have gotten away with it except my mother saw her from the attic window."

Roz saw the shocked look on Ford's face. "She didn't commit suicide." It was little consolation.

"That must be a relief to you," Lynette said. "Unfortunately, the two of you are the only people who know the truth. Everyone will think you couldn't live with your mother's suicide, Rozalyn, and took your own life. Sadly, your new boyfriend tried to save you. A terrible mistake on his part.''

''Lynette, the sheriff knows. You can't get away with this,'' Ford said. ''Killing more people isn't going to save you. And Drew, if I were you, I'd be hightailing it out of here. You don't have to take the rap for your mother anymore.''

Drew looked up from the blood-soaked handkerchief in his hand for a moment, then touched the wide open gash on his forehead, grimacing, too involved in his own pain now to even seem to realize what was happening.

Lynette shook her head as if amused by Ford's tactics. ''Drew is my *son*. He is all I have. He would never leave me. We will disappear again. I am very good at it and I have enough of Liam's money socked away. I will do just fine until I find another fool to charm into marriage. I really have had the worst luck with husbands dying on me.''

Another fool? Is that all Liam Sawyer was to her? Roz felt her face flame in anger. Ford must have seen it. He gave her a slight nod, then he stepped to the phonograph and kicked it hard.

The needle scratched loudly across the record. The plug jerked from the wall. The phonograph skidded loudly across the hardwood floor like a missile aimed right at Lynette.

It happened in a heartbeat. Lynette jumped back to avoid the phonograph flying toward her ankles. Roz saw her chance. She turned and grabbed the woman's wrist holding the gun and jerked her toward the open window of the widow's walk at the same time Roz bent down.

Drew, seeing what was happening, reached for his mother as Lynette began to fall over Roz toward the narrow widow's walk—and the four-story drop past the railing.

But Ford had already launched himself across the room, hitting Drew hard, chest-high. Drew's weapon clattered to the floor but his momentum drove him into his mother. It was just enough to propel Lynette into the widow's walk railing with Drew right behind her. Off balance, she hit the railing and would have gone over right then if she hadn't grabbed her son Drew's arm.

Roz got to her feet, turning in time to see both of their faces, Lynette's caught in a horrible grimace as she fought to save herself—even at the expense of her son. Drew's expression was one of realization. If his mother didn't let go, they would both go over the railing. Or with luck, his mother would be able to pull him over past her and save herself.

In that instant, Drew could either free himself of his mother—or take the brunt of the impact.

Lynette let go as Drew hit the top of the railing next to her. Roz heard the wood crack. Nothing could save him. He must have known that. His mother had regained her balance against a portion of the unbroken lower widow's walk railing. Relief washed over her expression and resignation as she watched her son start to go over the railing.

Roz watched in horror. To the end Drew had protected his mother.

At the very last minute, Drew grabbed his mother's sleeve. Roz saw the smile on his face and heard Lynette scream as the two plummeted over the side and dropped out of sight. Then Lynette's screams stopped with an abrupt silence that shook Roz to her core.

She turned to bury her face in Ford's shirt as he pulled her in his arms.

Epilogue

The days that followed were a blur. Ford had taken Roz straight to the hospital to see her father. Liam's eyes had widened, tears flooding them at the sight of her.

He'd drawn her into his arms and, although weak, he'd held her tightly. "I was so afraid they hurt you. Roz, I'm so sorry, so sorry."

"It wasn't your fault," she tried to reassure him.

"I was such a fool, such an old fool."

"You did it to get me home," she said.

He looked into her eyes. "Your mother would have so wanted us all here. I feel that in my heart. This is where your children should grow up. On this side of the Cascades, in the one place that made us all once happy."

Roz had felt Ford behind her. "I'm not sure I can do that, Dad."

"I understand," he said. "It was a foolish dream of mine. Forgive me?"

"There is nothing to forgive," she assured him.

It was later that she had learned Sheriff Mitch Tanner had been airlifted to Eugene with two gunshot wounds. Charity had been at his side.

His brother Jesse had taken over as deputy, show-ing up at Roz's house only moments after Drew and his mother had gone over the broken top railing of the widow's walk to their deaths in the garden below.

Roz and Ford had given him their statements a few days later. The woman she'd known as Emily Lane was in fact Lynette Hargrove. She had only one child, a son named Robert Hargrove Junior. The elderly Robert Hargrove Senior had died in his sleep with only his nurse Lynette, whom he'd recently married, in attendance. Unfortunately, his estate hadn't been as large as Lynette had hoped.

It would take months before all of Lynette's former husbands could be found because she had used so many different names.

The blonde Jesse found dead in the attic turned out to be a third-rate actress from Portland named Sunday Brooks. Her last act was as Suzanne Lane, one she no doubt would regret for eternity.

Roz spent that first night beside her father's bed along with Florie Jenkins. It wasn't until daylight that the nurse, Kate Clark, insisted the two go home and get some rest. She promised to watch over him for them.

Ford walked Roz out and offered to take her to breakfast. She'd declined. Nor had she wanted to go to the house. She'd taken a room at the Ho Hum. Ford had offered to get her things from the house. That was one offer she couldn't refuse.

Over the days that followed, she thought a lot about

what her father had asked her. Could she ever go back to that house? She felt torn between the years of happiness she'd known there and the horror. And yet the house was her last link to her mother.

She had come to grips with her mother's death, now at peace with the knowledge that her mother would never have left them the way she had if she'd had a choice.

The day before her dad was to be released from the hospital, he'd patted the side of his bed for her to sit. "I need to ask you what you want to do with the house. If you still feel the same way, I'll sell it and you'll never have to come back here. I'll go to Seattle and get a place up there closer to you. Just tell me what you want, sweetheart."

"Excuse me," Ford said from the doorway.

Roz turned and gave him an impatient look. Now was not the time to interrupt.

"We need to talk," Ford said. "Now." He looked past her to Liam. "You understand?"

"I don't understand," Roz said as Ford walked her out of the hospital.

"Liam does," he said and opened his pickup door for her.

"Where are we going? I thought you just wanted to talk? Why can't we talk right here?"

"Get in, Roz." It was the first time he'd called her that.

She slid in, her heart hammering so hard she just knew he could hear it. He had been there for her over the days since the attic, but not once had he tried to kiss her, or make love to her, or even say anything about the afternoon they'd spent in a cave in the Cascades.

"I'm hungry," he said as he slid behind the wheel.

She watched in amazement as he drove to Betty's and got out. She followed him, not knowing what else to do. Was this his idea of talking?

Only a few locals were in the café. She told herself she wasn't hungry. Her stomach was in knots. She figured Ford just wanted to tell her he was leaving. Why couldn't he just do that in the hospital hallway?

The smell of freshly baked pies drifted through the air. "I'll take a piece of banana cream," she told Betty, surprising herself. But she remembered something Charity had told her about banana cream pie.

Ford lifted a brow, then ordered an omelette. "Banana cream pie for breakfast?" he inquired.

She nodded. "It works for my friend, Charity." Hand trembling, she took a bite of the pie Betty slid in front of her and closed her eyes. Nothing. Just darkness behind her eyelids.

"Rozalyn?"

She opened her eyes, disappointed.

"There is something I didn't tell you."

She held her breath.

"When I was nine, my dad, my biological dad, John Wells, took me back into the Cascades with him on one of his Bigfoot searches. He left me alone while he climbed up to check out a cave. I saw something." He glanced toward the window. She followed his gaze to the dark green of the forest just across the street and beyond, miles and miles of wilderness. "I saw a huge creature covered with hair. It was watching me from the foliage. I have never been so terrified in my life.''

He shifted his gaze back to her face. ''That is, until I came into that attic and saw that woman holding a gun to your head.''

She stared at him, not sure which revelation shocked her the most. ''So you have known all along that Bigfoot exists?''

He looked surprised, then laughed. ''I'm trying to tell you something here.''

''You wanted my father's photographs to prove Bigfoot existed.''

He blinked. ''Yeah, I guess I did and when they didn't— Listen, I'm having a hard enough time saying this—''

''You came up here hoping for Bigfoot bones. I know how disappointed you must be,'' she said. ''But you wouldn't have sold them to the highest bidder.''

He stared at her. ''How do you know that?''

She smiled. ''I know.''

He laughed again and ran a hand over his hair to brush it back from his forehead. ''I guess I'll never know but once I met you—''

''That's why you never went with your father again, isn't it?'' she said suddenly, excited. ''You never told him what you saw! And he never understood why—''

He pushed off the booth, standing to lean over the table and kiss her.

She gasped in surprise.

''That is the only way I've found to shut you up,'' he said. ''I heard what your father said about your mother and the house. I have to know something. Do you think you could live there?''

She was still stunned by the kiss. ''What?''

''Let me put it this way. If I told you right now that I love you and don't want to spend a day of my life without you, would you want to stay in Timber Falls?''

She stared at him. ''Are you asking me—'' She couldn't bring herself to finish. She grabbed her fork, took a bite of her pie and closed her eyes tightly. And there he was. Ford Lancaster dressed in jeans and a flannel shirt sitting on the front steps of the Timber Falls house holding…holding a baby!

''Roz? In my inept way I'm trying to ask you to marry me and tell you that I'd stay here with you, if you'd have me. If it's what you want.''

Her eyes flew open. The look on his face made her laugh out loud. He really thought she might turn him down? Were all men fools at heart? ''Ford, oh Ford, yes!''

She slid from the booth to throw herself in his arms.

''Say the words, Rozalyn.''

And she said the words she thought she would never hear come out of her mouth. ''Ford Lancaster, I love you.''

OF COURSE, her father was ecstatic. Florie had been coming by every day to see how he was doing, as had Charity, who also had good news. Mitch had finally asked her to marry him and he was recovering nicely from his gunshot wounds.

Jesse had arrested Wade after his wounds had healed enough to leave the hospital. Daisy was filing for divorce. Their daughter Desiree was raising hell at the Duck Inn. Nothing new there, Charity said.

The evidence Roz and Ford had collected was turned over to Jesse. The DNA on the cigarette butts were compared to Drew's along with the tread on the boots. Both were a match. Drew had been doing his mother's dirty work since he was a boy so it came as no surprise he'd started the rock slide to kill Roz. Or that he'd staged the fake suicide at Lost Creek Falls.

Once Liam was well enough, he told Roz that a neighbor's dog had been digging in the garden and turned up the bones. That dog, Liam swore, had saved his life. If he hadn't found the old bones, he was certain that Emily, as he knew her, would have poisoned him.

He'd had doubts almost immediately about his hasty marriage. But when he'd found the bones, then later discovered rat poison in a drawer in the kitchen, he'd made that call to Roz. He had planned to get a divorce. But Emily wasn't going to let him leave. He'd confronted her. Of course, she'd denied everything. He had told her he had contacted his lawyer and that if anything should happen to him, like a poisoning, she would be the first person the police would come looking for. He'd tried to leave, but of course, Drew stopped him.

As it was, she drugged him, obviously realizing she had to move fast. He pretended to be out, then got to the phone. When he couldn't reach the sheriff, he'd hit redial since he could barely see. It was John

Wells's number. That's why he'd sounded like he was drunk.

Then Drew had hit him with something. It was the last thing he remembered. He wasn't surprised that Emily had come up with the story about him falling off a cliff. She would have gotten away with it, too, if it hadn't been for Roz coming to Timber Falls.

"Thank you," her dad had said, taking her hand. "I know how hard it was for you to come back here." He was saddened to hear that his old friend John Wells had died but he had known he was ill. "I'm just glad I got to meet his son," Liam said to Ford. "I owe you a huge debt for saving my daughter."

"It was my honor," Ford said. "I had a lot of practice. By the way, your truck and camper turned up. Some Bigfoot hunters found it hidden a few miles from here." He figured Emily had wanted him in the guest house so she and Drew could keep an eye on him. Her mistake.

The disk Ford had started writing his article on had also turned up in Drew's things. Drew had made a copy of the article and left it in the guest house that morning for Roz to find. As Roz watched, Ford had destroyed the disk and the article. She would never know what he had planned to do before he came to Timber Falls. All she knew was that she loved him and he loved her, and anyone who knew anything knew that love transformed a person. Charity Jenkins would attest to that. Mitch Tanner, too.

Roz and Ford went over to her house later that day. Roz stared at the place. Funny, it looked different now that it was empty. Ford had seen that everything had been cleaned out that would even remind her of her former stepfamily. The house looked a little sad to her. Like a house just crying out for a family that could love it.

Ford took her around to the back. The widow's walk was gone. He'd hired some carpenters with her father's approval to remove it. And the garden was being plowed up. The state investigation lab had been forced to dig up most of it just in case any more bodies were buried there.

Fortunately there weren't.

"I'm thinking a swimming pool," Ford said looking at the torn-up ground.

Roz nodded. She liked that idea. She turned to look back at the house. She knew she would grieve her mother's death wherever she lived, but here, she could hold on to all those years of wonderful memories. Here she could make new memories with her own family, her own children. And Charity's, she thought with a smile. Her mother and father had always thought Roz's and Charity's children would play here just as their mothers had.

Yes, Roz could see that happening—and maybe sooner than anyone thought.

"The first thing is paint, inside and out, bright colors," she said. "And big pots of flowers for the front porch. And we should throw a party. Yes," she said warming to the idea. "This town needs a party after everything that has happened."

Ford smiled over at her. "That's my girl."

She took his hand and they walked back toward the house. She could already hear the animated voices echoing through the old place, and almost hear hers and Ford's children running through the long hallways, laughing and calling to each other. Yes, this house would again ring with laughter. She and Ford would see to it.

It was strange but as Roz entered the house, she felt a warm breeze touch her cheek. She stopped and in that instant, she felt her mother's hand on her shoulder and heard her mother whisper in her ear, "Welcome home, dear."

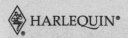

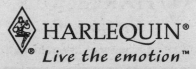

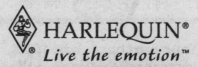

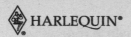

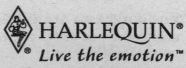

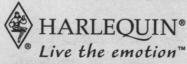

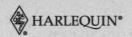

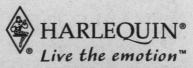